LOST SECRETS

A MYSTERY NOVEL

by

JOAN CARSON & PAMELA CURTISS

LOST SECRETS

ISBN: 978-0-692-11606-7

Cover Design by Cassie Raub

This is a work of fiction. All of the characters, organizations, and events portrayed in this novel are either products of the Authors imagination or used fictitiously.

Special thanks to Karle and Andi Bartholomew for insight into Scotland, and Shirley Miller for insight into England and her editing assistance.

First Edition

Printed in the United States of America

*Dedicated to Journalists everywhere
who are in search of the truth*

CHAPTER 1

July 1, 1945, Newbury, Berkshire, England

Natalie moved carefully from room to room, pulling up the blinds and tying back the curtains. She peered with lovely green eyes through the windows onto the private rear garden and its beautiful, picturesque views of the open countryside. The house was secluded, no other house being visible in summer from any of its windows. She was alone, waiting for her brother, Kenneth, to come home. He had gone to London the day before and was due to arrive home this morning. He went to conduct some secretive business affairs or at least that's what she suspected, because he refused to tell her anything about why he was traveling there. He often went to London on business and to socialize with his many friends and family, usually staying several days.

It was a clear morning and Natalie hoped it would remain sunny and bright all day. Rainy days could bring on headaches, and she was tired of the dull pain they would cause. Bruises and lacerations on her face had healed and were no longer visible, but she was glad there hadn't been any visitors. She feared she'd become a bit of a recluse, but knew she needed time to heal. She had been in a London hospital for several weeks and only at the country house for a few months.

The beautifully preserved five-bedroom cottage was decorated simply. It had been built in the late 1800's, with polished wood floors and wood beams crossing the high ceilings. Natalie had bought some houseplants recently and they were thriving on a bookcase which faced a south window. The new sprouts and buds symbolized hope and a bright new future for her, how all living things eventually heal, and how perseverance is a universal trait. If plants can carry on despite being damaged, she could as well.

She walked over to the fireplace in the living room and glanced at a picture of Kenneth on the mantel, so handsome, in a tailored light-colored linen suit. She took the picture and held it in her hands. He looked so carefree and innocent. Clearly the picture was taken before the war. Such an upstanding young gentleman, so strong and healthy, no wonder he became one of the top pilots for the RAF and made his family proud.

Placing the picture back on the mantel, she walked across to the door leading into the drawing room. It creaked as she moved it back and forth. She would need to talk to Kenneth about it and have it repaired. She wondered why Kenneth chose to live here in this isolated place when he enjoyed the London life so much. A single young man should be enjoying the excitement that London had to offer. He said she could join him on one of his trips to London as soon as she was feeling better. That was something she was looking forward to.

She was also looking forward to seeing her parents again. They had been abroad during the time of her hospital stay, Kenneth had said, and would be back soon. Of course, they had called for updates on her recovery.

The chimes on the door startled her. She was puzzled that someone would be at their door; it was barely 9 o'clock and she'd just finished breakfast. This was the first visitor to the house since she had arrived.

She opened the door to find a distinguished-looking gentleman with a serious manner about him. He looked at her and then glanced through the doorway at the room inside.

"Good morning miss. I am Detective Inspector Spencer from Scotland Yard. Is Kenneth Michaels in? This is his house, is it not?"

"Yes, this is his house but no, he's not here," Natalie said apprehensively. She was certainly not expecting a detective to show up at the door and was more than a little surprised. An inkling of danger briefly crossed her thoughts, and she hoped this man wasn't bringing bad news.

"Do you know when he will be home?"

"I expect him this morning but I'm not sure what time. Was he expecting you?"

"We had arranged to meet next week at my office in London but as I was out this way I thought I would drop in. Mind if I wait for him?"

Detective Spencer was a large, thick-set man with soft features and thinning gray hair. He offered a reassuring smile after seeing the concern on Natalie's face.

"Of course, you may wait for him. Please come in."

Spencer gave her an inquisitive, rather lingering look as he stepped inside the door. Such an intense scrutiny made her uneasy. He felt her discomfort and looked down after a moment as he closed the door behind him and followed her into the room. Then she stopped, turned and looked at him, her face a complete question mark.

"What is this about?"

"Well, miss, it's about a murder."

"Murder. I haven't heard anything about a murder. Here in Newbury?"

"No, in London some years ago, before the war. It seems there is more to the murder than what it appeared to be at the time. It's being investigated again because of some new information we've received. It was determined the case would be better off in the hands of Scotland Yard rather than the local authorities so it has been turned over to me." He hoped this would partially satisfy her.

Spencer looked at the beautiful woman in front of him and couldn't help noticing her exquisite green eyes, the likes of which he had never seen before, and she seemed very kind and cordial. If this was Ken's fiancé, he was indeed a lucky man.

"Please sit down," she suggested, as she led the way into the living room and gestured toward a comfortable leather chair.

"Thank you."

"You must be tired if you've travelled from London. That is where Kenneth has been since yesterday so, it seems like you just missed each other."

Natalie offered him a cigarette which he accepted. Spencer's gaze fixed upon her as he took it from her hand, pulled out a silver lighter, and lit it. He moved the ash tray on the adjacent small table toward him and took a long, slow drag. Finally, he said, "May I ask who you are? Are you Ken's fiancé?"

"No," she said as she blushed slightly, "please forgive my manners." She extended her hand. "I am his sister, Natalie Michaels."

As Spencer took her hand his grip tightened and his eyes widened with a look of surprise on his face. Natalie could detect a change in his relaxed and friendly mood. He stared at her with a look of curiosity and extreme intensity which made Natalie uncomfortable.

"Who are you, miss?" he asked again, "I think I misheard you."

"Natalie Michaels," she answered in a casual and light tone of voice wondering why he would find it unusual that Kenneth's sister was in his house. He finally let go of her hand, which she was very glad to get back. She wasn't sure how to handle this unexpected visitor who seemed so interested in her. He would probably enjoy some refreshment. Perhaps food would distract him.

"Can I get you anything, would you like some tea and biscuits?"

"Some tea would be nice, thank you," he answered without taking his gaze off of her.

"Milk and sugar as well?"

"Yes, thank you."

Natalie left the room to put the tea kettle on. When she came back, Spencer was deep in thought. He looked like he wanted to say something but couldn't find the words.

"Are you alright? You look quite pale," she asked.

"Perfectly all right."

They sat in silence until the tea kettle whistled indicating the water was ready. Natalie again left the room and returned carrying a tray laden with the teapot, milk in a small ceramic pitcher, sugar, two cups and biscuits. She carefully poured the tea into the cups and handed one to the detective.

"Thank you," he said as he took the cup and added one spoonful of sugar and a smidgeon of milk. He stirred them in thoughtfully.

Natalie sat down and took a sip of tea. It was starting to feel quite awkward with this detective not saying anything and just staring at her.

"Who was murdered?" she asked casually.

"You, miss."

Lost Secrets

CHAPTER 2

She looked at the inspector, completely astonished and speechless. Spencer considered himself to be a good judge of character and while realizing something deceptive was going on, his first instinct was that this woman was not part of it.

At that moment, outside the house, Kenneth Michaels returned from London to a very disturbing sight. He saw a strange, official-looking car parked in front of his country home and knew that meant trouble. No visitors were expected or wanted. What was he going to walk into?

As he entered the house, two pairs of eyes stared at him.

"I can explain," Kenneth said.

****

Natalie looked confused and was leaning back in her chair. Spencer had a quizzical look on his face, waiting for clarification on this matter which was becoming more interesting by the minute.

Even though she was relieved to see Kenneth, her voice came across unstable as she said, "Kenneth, this is Detective Inspector Spencer from Scotland Yard."

Kenneth was stunned. "What a surprise. I thought we had arranged an appointment at your office next week."

"Well, I'm here today, aren't I? Spencer was a bit annoyed as he had expected a casual visit and didn't like surprises. It was damn good luck he had chosen to stop in today.

"Indeed you are."

"And you know why I'm here. To talk to you about investigating the murder of your sister, Natalie, who seems to have just served me tea."

He gave Kenneth an accusing look and lifted his eyebrows, waiting for an answer that would make sense concerning the woman in the room.

"I understand, sir, and I see how this looks."

"Please tell me, how does it look?"

"It looks bad, but I am prepared to disclose everything," Kenneth said as he sat down in one of the large leather chairs and exhaled slowly. This was not in his plans. He realized it was time to come clean, it was time to tell the truth.

Keeping his eyes on the woman in front of him, he said to Spencer, "This lovely lady who sits across from us has amnesia from a traumatic head injury. Obviously, she is not my sister, Natalie."

She looked at him, staring, as she said in a barely audible voice, "Well then, who am I?" She could not believe what she was hearing. Why had he lied to her and who was she?

"I will explain everything to you." His tone was gentle as he turned toward her, concern showing on his face and his eyes seemed to say he was sorry that she found out like this, without him being able to prepare her.

Kenneth looked back again to Spencer. "Detective, could you leave us alone for a bit, come back later perhaps, or I will meet you at your office another time? I need to talk with her, and as you have surmised, I have a lot to explain and would appreciate some privacy. Believe me, I will come clean with you and do everything I can to help in the investigation of my sister's murder. I am more than happy that the investigation is in the capable hands of Scotland Yard."

Spencer was far too curious to walk away at this point.

"Absolutely not! I want to hear the explanation now. It's my duty to find out what is going on here."

Kenneth struggled to come up with the right words.

"All right then, here it is. In Germany, this woman, whose name is Kate, saved me and my men from an unexpected enemy attack. She came to us and warned us, with no regard for her own safety. She took a considerable risk. While helping us escape, she received a serious head injury from enemy artillery and was knocked unconscious. Reinforcements came to take the wounded to England. I wanted to make sure she was in safe hands so I took her identification and replaced it with Natalie's passport. I had carried the passport and Natalie's locket with me since her murder as a reminder that I needed to survive the war to someday help bring her killer to justice." He paused to take a breath and gather his thoughts. The seconds turned into minutes as he sat deep in reflective thought.

"Don't leave us hanging, this is most intriguing," Spencer said, trying to control his anxious curiosity and not wanting to miss any part of the story.

"She was brought to a London hospital, as Natalie Michaels. As I've said, Kate has amnesia and no memory of the attack or who she is. And, right now she has no idea why she is at my house. I brought her here to recuperate and told her she was my sister in order to avoid causing her undue concern during her recovery. I've been trying to find out more about her background in the meantime. If you would please allow me a few moments to talk with her alone and give her a chance to recover from the shock of finding out she's not my sister, I promise to be at your service, detective."

Satisfied with this remarkable explanation and with consideration for the young woman in the room, Spencer acquiesced and reluctantly stood up, put on his hat and walked toward the door. Kenneth followed him to his car.

Alone in the sitting room, Kate moved to the ottoman and sat down, totally distraught, staring into space as if trying to comprehend what she had just heard.

Outside in the fresh air, the story still sounded absurd. Standing beside Spencer, leaning against his car, Kenneth reluctantly continued his story. "Her full name is Katherine Richter. My father and I are trying to figure out her history and her involvement in the war."

"Good heavens, man. Why on earth would you do this? This is an extraordinary breach of conduct."

"Because she saved my life and that of my men and was wounded seriously herself. I guess I felt I owed it to her. It was obvious to me that she was working for the Allies. She said she was and gave me no cause not to believe her. Left in Germany, she would have been captured and shot." He paused. "Or worse." He looked Spencer straight in the eyes. "Could I really leave her there?"

Spencer nodded slowly. With his suspicions calmed down a bit, his face softened and reflected a look of understanding. Or maybe it was sympathy.

Kenneth added, "Perhaps you could help. I would be in your debt, sir, if you could find out anything you can about her identity, using whatever available resources you have at the Yard or any other means at your disposal."

Spencer reluctantly indicated he would try to help in the matter. "I came here for help to solve a mystery and now you are asking for my help to investigate another."

"Yes, I know it's asking a lot, but it would be a tremendous help. And I will assist in every way possible to investigate the murder of my sister."

Spencer gave him a long, searching look, then got in his car and drove off. Kenneth did not relish the idea of going back into the house. He was very upset that Kate had found out she was not his sister in this cold and unfeeling way. Damn the detective!

CHAPTER 3

London, England, April 2, 1945

Katherine Richter lay in a hospital bed recovering from a serious concussion and suffering from physical and psychological trauma due to injuries received during a heavy artillery attack in Germany. However, she was not aware of this as she opened her eyes one Saturday morning. She didn't even know her name and only knew where she was, who she was, and what year it was because she had been told by hospital staff. The man sitting next to her bed held her hand.

"Who are you?" she inquired. Everything seemed so fuzzy and distant. This man was very handsome with dark hair and striking blue eyes. She wondered why he was taking an interest in her.

"I'm your brother, Ken." This was the first time that anyone had talked to her except for hospital staff, who had been very kind. She had seen other patients come and go but no-one had visited her.

"I'm sorry. I don't remember you. You're my brother?" Could it be true that she had a family?

"You have amnesia, no memory of who you are. You were wounded in an enemy attack and have been in a coma and are now here in a London hospital." He took her hand. "The war will be over very soon."

"What attack? Will I be okay?"

"You'll be okay," he said reassuringly.

Kate smiled as Ken gently moved a strand of her hair out of her face as he said, "The doctors here have done a great job stitching the cut on your face. It has almost completely healed and it doesn't look like you'll have a scar."

"Where do I live?"

"You live with me in the country. Your name is Natalie Michaels. Our parents are in Scotland, but they call every day to ask how you are doing. We all love you very much. I'll answer all your questions, I promise, but right now the doctor says you must get some rest. You'll be discharged soon and will come home with me to our country cottage. Until then, they will take good care of you here." He smiled, released her hand and stood up to leave.

Kate's eyes felt heavy and she closed them, wondering if she'd just had a dream. She hoped her brother would return again soon.

Watching her fall back to sleep, Kenneth left the room and walked into an adjoining consulting room. He greeted his good friend, Doctor David Wells, a well-respected physician who specialized in wartime trauma.

"What have you found out about her?" Kenneth asked.

"I'm working on that. I have asked my source at the University administration office to find out information about a Katherine Richter, not mentioning that she is in this hospital under the name of Natalie Michaels. I just told him she was a friend of my cousin and she was wondering what happened to her."

"It's a good thing she's speaking English, isn't it?"

"Yes, it is, speaking German here at this time would not go over well. I've done some research about her, as you have asked and learned that Katherine attended school here in London. But there is no doubt she is quite fluent in German as well as it is her native language. She is speaking English because everyone is speaking to her in English. Memories of language and motor skills such as walking would not be something that an amnesiac would forget."

"But why doesn't she have a German accent?"

"We aren't speaking to her with a German accent. No doubt she learned to speak English without a German accent since she was educated here."

"When will her memory come back?"

12

"It's hard to say. Most people with amnesia do regain their memory, slowly over time."

"Have you found out anything else about her?"

"Yes, I'm sorry to tell you that my source, someone who attended the University that Katherine attended, indicated Katherine went back to Germany before the war and he assumed she became a member of the Third Reich. He thinks that she would have been a valuable resource to them for translation purposes, since she spoke English and French as well as German."

Seeing the frown on Kenneth's face, Doctor Wells added, "I don't know how reliable my source is, if that makes you feel better. There are no official records yet. I would say he is mostly just surmising and has a strong prejudice as well, against everyone German."

"You could never convince me that she worked for them," Kenneth said with spite and disgust in his voice.

"Why is that?"

"She saved my life and that of my men. She warned us of an imminent enemy raid, she knew details of where and when. She did so at her own risk. I believe she was an allied spy, probably recruited by MI5. She was injured in the raid but saved us. Thanks to her, we had no casualties."

"It's also possible she changed sides near the end, realizing that the Allies would be victorious. She is a very beautiful woman. Are you sure you aren't blinded by that? Are you willing to accept the truth about her, whatever that might be?"

"I know what I know," Kenneth said with determination and certainty in his voice.

"Do you have feelings for this woman?"

Kenneth took a moment and thought carefully before answering. "No, the thought hadn't entered my mind. You're right, I don't really know her. But I do want to find out the truth about her, but not from some prejudiced, disreputable and vague source, rather from real classified information that we probably won't have access to until after the war."

"Now I understand more about why you arranged for her to be brought here. Great cover, the name on the passport found on her is Natalie Michaels. And a locket with the initials of NM. I imagine you had something to do with that."

"I did."

"You're lucky I'm such a good friend, allowing her to be known as your sister. No one is questioning that she is not Natalie Michaels. No one at the hospital would be aware that Natalie was murdered at the start of the war. And as luck would have it, she looks a lot like Natalie. Amazingly, she has green eyes, what are the odds of that?"

"Kismet, I guess. She would have died if I left her in Germany, either from her head wound, as she was bleeding profusely, or if the German army had found her and they pieced together why she was there. As I've told you, she saved me and my men. I couldn't just leave her there. Wouldn't you have done something for her if she'd just saved your life?"

Wells didn't answer and after a slight pause, said "Well, so far, your plan worked. Everyone here in the hospital thinks she's Natalie Michaels. We'll keep it that way. Otherwise she'll be discharged to a POW camp or held as a German spy. There is a lot of anti-German sentiment around and a thirst for revenge."

"Yes, I am quite aware of that."

"Not to mention the trouble that you would be in, bringing in a German national."

Kenneth looked thoughtfully at Wells. He had often felt concern for the risk he had taken with his actions. It had been a spur-of-the-moment decision made under pressure during wartime, but he was the kind of person to follow his instincts. They had always proven him right. At least so far.

"Yes, I know, and I'll take responsibility for my actions, if it comes to that. I've told my parents and brother about the ruse. They're the only ones who know about it, beyond you and me. I can't say they are happy about it, but they're glad I came home from the war in one piece. I want to take Kate home with me as soon as you'll release her. I have a cottage in the country that I often use for summer holidays. It's isolated and it will be safe for her until we work things out. Eventually I'll tell her who she is once she's better and we find out more about her. Until then, I'll look after her. This bloody war will be over soon enough."

Lost Secrets

CHAPTER 4

After the Detective's visit, July 1, 1945, Newbury, Berkshire, England

Sitting alone on the couch with Kenneth and Spencer outside, Kate admitted to a sense of relief. She had held suspicions after arriving at the cottage that she might not be Kenneth's sister. So many things had been unclear and unexplained. Although he had been very kind, she hadn't wanted to confront or question him. It was hard enough to get through a given day, not knowing her own history and with jumbled thoughts. There was never a good time to say anything about her concerns and she didn't know how to word them.

Once, she found a dress in the back of the closet in her room which did not fit her well. It was a bit too long and a little loose in the shoulders and waist. She could understand that she may have lost weight, but the woman who owned the dress was a few inches taller than her. When she showed it to Kenneth, he immediately took it and said it must have been left by a visitor years ago. He had purchased new clothes and shoes for her as soon as they'd left the hospital, telling her he wanted her to have the latest styles. She didn't question his generosity.

She continuously wished she knew more about how she had been injured and how she got to the hospital. Kenneth had given her vague details about being in a place where a bomb had exploded. When she asked for more information, he always told her he didn't want to upset her, because the doctors said stress would cause her to get worse.

And it had seemed disheartening that her mother or father hadn't come to see her, stopped their travels. It seemed that most parents would be rushing to her side in her time of need. Kenneth said they loved her but didn't want to disrupt her until she was ready.

She had also noticed there were no pictures in the cottage of her or of Kenneth and her together, only the picture of him. She didn't have any friends apparently, or they would have come by to visit. The people she had met in the town were very friendly but didn't act like they knew her, only meeting her for the first time, but of course most of the people she met were all new to the area themselves. New employment opportunities had arisen toward the end of the war and she understood many had left London, disillusioned.

Townsfolk were all very kind and she had made some several acquaintances. She had gone to the market with Kenneth for groceries and started making recipes from a cookbook she found in the kitchen. Besides working on cooking, she spent her days reading books and magazines that he would buy for her, trying to find out more about current events and the war that had devastated Europe and the world. When Kenneth was home, they would play board games and enjoy each other's company.

Except for him, she felt pretty much alone in the world. And in the back of her mind were blurry thoughts and figures of men and women that stayed in the background of her consciousness. She didn't know what to do with them and never mentioned them to Kenneth.

And, of course there were the headaches. At times a very sharp, strong pain would stab at her and she would need to lie down with the curtains closed. Laying in the dark for hours, she would struggle to remove all thoughts from her mind and try to relax. Other times it was a slight ache that would dull her senses. Kenneth seemed to leave her alone much of the time, and she didn't want him to be worried about her.

Now much of this was explained. She had been deceived about her identity. What Kenneth had told the detective about her sounded complicated and like someone else's life, but it did make sense, all the secrecy and seclusion. Why was Kenneth keeping her here? Was he really trying to help her? It would be good to know the truth but part of her feared what the complete truth would be. If he was telling the truth, it would be a relief to know she'd done some good in this world before her injury, and that she'd had a life of her own.

The front door banged shut and Kenneth returned to the living room. He looked at her and in an apologetic voice said, "I am extremely sorry you had to find out this way, this was not supposed to happen. I was going to tell you soon." His eyes reflected genuine concern.

"Please, tell me more about who I am and what all this means. And why am I here?" Kate responded, in a much more natural voice than when Kenneth escorted out the detective. She had regained her composure and the color had returned to her face.

Kenneth sat down across from her and took her hand. "First of all, I need to ask for your forgiveness in not telling you the whole truth all these months."

"I forgive you," she responded, "I'm sure you had a good reason, but now please tell me everything you know about me."

"I'm not sure who exactly you are. I have been trying very hard to find out more about you. I know you were born and raised in Germany. Your parents were killed there before the war."

"My God! My parents were killed?"

"Yes, I'm afraid so, this was one of the reasons I didn't want to tell you about your past.

Your mother was a teacher. Your father fought in the Great War and worked in a factory. He had union ties. They probably got on the wrong side of the Nazi party, as many did. You are not married and were attending University in London when war broke out. I don't know if you have any siblings, but I haven't found any documentation that you do. Since you are a German citizen, I brought you here to keep you safe. Your full name is Katherine Richter."

Katherine Richter

Kate took back her hand and managed a sip of tea. "Please go on."

Kenneth told her the entire story of the events that happened in Germany and her subsequent stay at the London hospital, in greater detail than his brief explanation to Detective Spencer. As he spoke, she put her hand on the beautiful gold locket she constantly wore and held it, aware that it really no longer belonged to her and never had. What a series of remarkable circumstances were coming to light today, Kate thought as she listened to his story, and again felt a wave of relief in learning how she ended up in this isolated place.

"A fellow student at the University you were attending in London mentioned that you left for Germany at the start of the war and he concluded that you were working for the Third Reich, translating for them since you are fluent in English and French. To protect you, I brought you here and kept you in seclusion. This former student did not know you were here in England when we inquired about you."

*Helping the Nazis, no, that can't be. Please God, no. K*ate looked aghast. So much for her sense of comfort.

"Of course, I don't believe a word of it," Ken said with a determined voice and gentle kind eyes, seeing how much this had upset her.

"No! That's not possible! I may not know who I am, but I know what kind of person I am."

She couldn't have been working for the Third Reich. England seemed like her home. The Nazi's had done so many terrible things before and during the war. She knew she wasn't like them. More and more information about atrocities they did to the Jews and others in Germany and during their occupation in Poland, France and other countries they invaded were coming out and it was awful.

During her stay in the hospital and the country home, she read and heard on the radio about the unspeakable horrors of the Nazi Regime. She and everyone around her had felt a huge relief when England celebrated VE day and the war in Europe was over.

"It can't be true," Ken continued, "Why would you have saved me and my men if you were working with them? You took a great risk. It was a secret attack and information that few had privy to. The only thing that makes sense is that you were a spy working for the Allies, stationed in Germany."

"Thank you, yes that is very likely. I certainly would not have worked for them if they killed my parents, now would I?"

"No."

"I could understand, however, that I might be glad to work against them to help avenge their deaths."

"Very true. We will find out who you are. I will be with you every step of the way until your memory comes back. I owe you my life."

"How very kind." Kate managed a slight smile. "From what you have said, I guess I owe you my life as well."

"Do you remember anything about Germany?"

"Germany." Her vision blurred with tears.

Lilacs. The sun shining through tall trees. A man and a pretty woman playing with a small dog. Laughing as she joined in, feeling loved, safe with her family.

Kenneth gave Kate a handkerchief so that Kate could dab her eyes. After a few moments, Kenneth spoke again.

"Kate, a lot of my business in London has been researching your background. My parents and my brother know about you and what you've been through."

"We have a brother? I mean, you have a brother?"

Kate and Kenneth both laughed slightly, a little humor helped alleviate some of the tension. They had spent many evenings laughing together so this seemed natural to them and brought back a sense of normality.

"It may take a while for me to get used to not being your sister," Kate said, "Sorry, please go on."

"My father has been helping me find out more about you, since he works in government. None of my friends or other relatives know about you or that you are here."

21

'Right."

"Don't worry, you are safe here," he said as he put his hand gently over hers.

His touch felt different now that she knew she was not his sister. Kate got up and walked quietly past him over to the bathroom. She looked in the mirror and thought how strange it was to look at herself and not know who exactly was looking back. What now? She splashed water on her face and gently dried off. Then she opened the back door and looked out at the large sky stretching across the green and felt the slight breeze. The quiet countryside and few moments alone helped refresh her.

Returning to where Kenneth was sitting, she sat down and sipped her tea without saying another word about her identity. She wondered how long it would take for her memory to return. The doctor said it would come back in bits and pieces.

Looking at Kenneth and his obvious distress, her thoughts suddenly returned to the present and the encounter with Detective Spencer and the reason for his visit. Kenneth's sister had been murdered.

"Kenneth, I'm so sorry to hear about your sister. Please tell me more about Natalie. What happened to her?"

"She was murdered in London before the war, she was strangled. My parents and brother are still grieving as am I." He stopped for a moment and cleared his throat.

"I am so sorry," Kate said. "That must have been awful to go through."

"She was a beautiful and caring woman. We miss her terribly, her smile and her laugh. Everything about her was very special and she was not only my sister, but my best friend. She had green eyes like you. Natalie was engaged to be married to a family friend by the name of Andrew Cresswell. He joined the forces soon after she died."

"Did he survive the war?"

"Yes, he is back in London but suffering from shell shock. I think he witnessed some pretty awful things."

"So, they have never determined who killed Natalie?"

"No, they did not find out. They are re-investigating the case and I'm glad. It's been over five years and finding the culprit would give me and my family some needed closure. Not long after her murder, we were dragged into the war and I entered the RAF. I think the investigation went on the back-burner, so to speak, everything centered on the war effort and didn't get the attention it would have received under normal circumstances. My parents were very worried that they would lose me too. That is probably why they went along with this charade. They are very grateful to you. They are religious and believe that it was God's grace, through you, that I survived the war."

"It would have been tragic for them to lose you as well. Please tell me more about Natalie. Where was she, what was she doing?" Kate found it intriguing that she apparently looked like his sister, and her thoughts immediately moved toward helping him feel better. He seemed to have done a lot for her considering she was a stranger to him.

"I'll try to tell you about her, but it is hard to put into words her capacity for compassion and kindness, not to mention her integrity. She was working as a reporter in London for the society column of a newspaper."

"A reporter? She must have been intelligent and educated."

Ken hesitated, "Now that the Yard is investigating her murder, I wonder if it didn't have something to do with her work as a reporter and the impending war."

"Yes, that does seem a likely possibility."

Ken then told Kate everything about Natalie and the circumstances surrounding her murder.

Lost Secrets

Chapter 5

London, England, September 24, 1939

Natalie was worried. She recently had the sense that someone was watching her, following her. Living in London while the country had just declared war on Germany was worrisome enough without a feeling of treachery looming about. It was fall of 1939 and things looked bleak as the nation prepared for battle. Her job as a reporter at *The Daily Mirror* had also become difficult.

Her friend, Jolene, often complained to her that "Nothing is ever easy" and it was so true. Jolene was always having difficulties, mostly brought on by herself. She never took the time to consider whether something made logical sense, she instead only followed her heart.

Natalie was often the same way. Her fiancé, Andrew, was difficult at times, and she never felt secure that he totally loved her as much as she loved him. He was unpredictable and she was surprised when he proposed marriage. They had been dating for three years and Natalie was about to give up on him. Once a month or so, they would sneak off together to his quaint small cottage, some ten kilometers northwest of where he was living. He would pick her up at the train station with open arms. During these times, they spent romantic days and nights together, always laughing and enjoying each other's company. Natalie was truly in love with Andrew.

She spent a moment thinking back to when he surprised her, three months ago. They were walking side by side in the trees behind his cottage when he suddenly stopped.

"Natalie, I have something to say to you."

She felt a pull in her gut, concerned he was going to tell her he was seeing someone else, or that he didn't love her anymore.

Taking a deep breath, she responded with, "Okay, I'm all ears."

He turned her towards him, putting his hands on her shoulders, looking her straight in the eyes.

"This is hard for me to put into words, but you need to know. I am hoping you'll say yes."

"Yes, to what?" She was still unsure of the direction he was heading.

"Will you marry me?"

Her heart melted as he pulled her towards him and they kissed and hugged for a full five minutes. It was beautiful, it was wonderful, she had never experienced such a thrilling moment in her life. Their relationship had further blossomed as friends and family found out about the engagement and planning for the wedding had started. Now she didn't have to lie to her uncle anymore about where she was going on those weekends with Andrew. She supposed it was a bit scandalous to spend nights with him, but that's how she was, not afraid to follow her feelings, and her uncle understood, having once been in love himself.

But now her job was really starting to wear her down. Her boss had assigned her to investigate some rumors about members of the highest levels of society who weren't being as supportive as hoped toward the war effort. Some people were impressed by the efficiency of the Nazi regime or they had business ties to Germany. Others were out-right spies. Natalie came from a wealthy family, and often attended parties and soirees with political men and their wives. She was supposed to act carefree and easy at these occasions but somehow ask loaded questions that might give some clue as to anyone that could be a potential problem for the government. She did all this while she wrote her usual column covering glamorous society events

She was considered glamorous herself by all who knew her, but humility kept her from acknowledging her effect on the men around her. Jolene tried, but could not compete with Natalie for attention and recognition which lead to an undercurrent of jealousy and contempt within their otherwise close friendship.

Natalie felt fortunate to have a job and enjoyed being a career woman. She hoped to make a difference in a world becoming increasing volatile. She had been saving her earnings in preparation of what looked like an uncertain future. Her uncle, Sir Frederick Michaels, had a large house on the outskirts of London, not too far from the *Mirror,* and he generously let her live on the main floor for a pittance, as she insisted on paying. Her uncle had never married, although he was quite handsome (she thought) and with the hired staff onboard, she could focus on her career and her mission. The cook and housekeeper, Anna, prepared their meals, and a young man, Travis, took care of the garden, acted as chauffer and valet, and did almost every other odd job that needed to be done.

The house was comfortably furnished with Victorian oak furniture and Natalie felt safe there. Her bedroom was on the back side of the building on the main floor. Next to her bedroom was a room that was set up as an office, with French doors which led out to a patio and the garden. The small yard was fenced on all sides, with a latching gate where one could head out to an alley. It offered privacy for them when they entertained outside on the patio. The garden contained numerous rosebushes and a large willow tree.

After her reverie about the engagement and the wedding planning, Natalie was back at her typewriter. It was 9 o'clock in the evening and she was tired, but she still had some notes to type up from the day. Earlier that afternoon she had posted a letter to her brother, Ken, who was currently still staying at his summer country cottage in Newbury. Some information she had accidentally come across was deeply troubling her, and he was the only person she could trust to discuss it with. In her letter, she didn't mention any details but begged him to come to London as soon as he could, to talk to him in person. Ken was such a bright spot in her life and she missed him when he wasn't nearby.

Lost Secrets

She typed intently, working to finish another letter, this one to her friend and colleague, Dexter Flynn. She looked up from her work, and randomly glanced out the door, noticing the back gate appeared unlatched. That was unusual, since she was sure she had closed it securely when she came home. Her uncle was out of town for a few days and the staff had gone home for the night as well. It was dark, and she couldn't tell but it looked different somehow.

Signing the letter, she got up and opened the glass doors, stepping outside into the darkened garden. Walking through the shadows, she reached the gate, when she heard movement behind her. Before she had a chance to turn around, strong hands gripped her throat and there was no escape from the pain as her breath and life drained out onto the carefully clipped grass.

CHAPTER 6

July 2, 1945, London, England

After a wait of 45 minutes, Detective Spencer was finally summoned into the Colonel's office at the military building, second floor Room 216. He hoped to hear some useful information to help Kenneth Michaels with his strange request so that he could move on to his other case. It was late morning and Spencer had an afternoon meeting to attend back at his office.

"Detective, I regret to inform you that I am unable to find out any information about this woman, Katherine Richter. However, I would suggest you talk to a friend of mine who works at MI5,' Colonel Horning said. "His name is David Nelson and he may be able to help you. I believe he worked with some of the covert counterespionage going on in France and Germany. If you mention my name and tell him that I referred you to him, he'll be more likely to give you information."

"I appreciate that," Spencer responded. He'd take any referrals he could to get into MI5.

The Colonel was a man with no pretenses and he always came straight to the point. "How did you say you met this woman?"

"It involves a case I'm working on." The two stared at each other, with Spencer being the more stubborn of the two. "I can't divulge anything more than that."

Horning conceded, and Spencer took down the number of the agent, David Nelson, and thanked the Colonel for his time. Driving back to his own office at Scotland Yard, he felt at least some sense of hope. A cold murder case hadn't sounded that interesting, but now there was a new angle. Solving it and uncovering information about this woman, Kate, intrigued him.

The next morning Spencer arrived at the office in a hopeful mood. His office was well kept and orderly with a few personal items, including a photograph of him and his family. He sat down at his desk and considered whether he should pursue this further. He had told Kenneth Michaels he would conduct research and now he was curious as well. What story would he tell Nelson as to why he needed the information? Would Nelson want to know more details of the case he was working on?

Apprehensively he called the agent with his request for information regarding Katherine Richter, letting him know that he was referred to him by Colonel Horning. He told him he needed to know if Katherine was a British operative and that it was essential to a murder case he was working on. To his surprise, Nelson did not ask further questions but said he was reluctant to release any highly classified information. Spencer reiterated that the information was critical to help him solve a murder, and appealed to his sense of justice now that the world was 'getting back to normal' with the end of the war in Europe. After a few tense moments, eventually Nelson acquiesced and said he would investigate if Katherine was an allied agent and then call him back.

Spencer did not know at the time if he was speaking the truth – whether the knowledge he requested would lead to solving the murder of Natalie Michaels. He leaned forward in his chair, took off his glasses and rubbed his eyes, hoping he would not face consequences from his superiors for this unprecedented request. He continued with other paperwork, hoping Nelson would provide this important information.

It seemed ages before the phone rang and Spencer was just about to leave for another meeting. He snatched the phone up, listening intently. Nelson confirmed that Katherine Richter was a British Agent. She worked undercover as a secretary and interpreter for German Intelligence but intercepted and changed secret dispatches to mislead the Nazis. He wasted no time in phoning Kenneth to tell him the good news.

CHAPTER 7

"What splendid news! You can go back to living your life," Kenneth said to Kate as he put down the phone. They were just about to sit down to a light lunch that Kate had prepared. Joy and relief showed on his face and in his tone. No longer did he have to worry about the culpability of his actions. "Detective Spencer has confirmed with MI5 that you were a British agent working for us in Germany."

"That's wonderful. Thank you." Kate was pleased to hear confirmation of her allied involvement and reassurance that she had not been working for the Nazis. She felt better about herself and her future immediately. Now she could start work on forming her own sense of identity, a woman of honor who did what she could to help the allied forces to victory. Kenneth was relieved as well, since he had been in a precarious situation from his actions.

Kate then thought about what was in store for her now. What would she do and where would she go? As if reading her thoughts, Kenneth said, "You may stay here as long as you wish. I can help you find employment and a place to live. We can research people here in England that you knew and find out more about your past. You went to school in London so maybe you have relatives here in England and I'm sure, many friends."

"Thank you, that is so very kind of you. I wonder though, how many of my classmates from before the war will think the same way that your source did, that I left London to go to Germany to join the Nazi party. I might be better off making a fresh start. You've done so much for me. How can I ever repay you?"

"You already saved my life."

Kate was holding back tears of joy. She had a million ideas going through her head for a future - now that she was free to have a future. She owed so much to Ken for getting her safely out of Germany and medical treatment at a London hospital. He was a handsome and self-sufficient man, but even men sometimes could benefit from the help of a woman.

She then realized how she could help repay Kenneth for his kindness to her. If she'd been a spy, she must be good at researching and sorting through facts and solving issues.

"I want to help you and Detective Spencer with the investigation of Natalie's murder," Kate announced.

Kenneth was taken aback by the suggestion. He stumbled for an answer.

"Thanks for the offer but you don't want to get involved in it. Best to leave it to the professionals."

"Really, Ken, it's not in your nature to just 'leave it to the professionals'. I don't believe that. I know you and I'm certain you are planning on investigating the murder yourself, with or without help from the detective."

"Yes, you know me well, but it could become dangerous and I don't want you involved."

"Dangerous? If I was an undercover agent in Germany during a ruthless regime that used to shoot spies on a thread of evidence with no trial, or so I've read, I must have the ability to deal with danger and the skills to read people. Otherwise I probably would not be alive at this moment."

"Well, you've got a good point." He looked at Kate thoughtfully. "A cousin of mine is getting married a week from Saturday in London. I was going to stay at my uncle's house there, on the outskirts of London, and ask around. Many of my sister's friends and family will be at the wedding and a lot of after-wedding parties are planned. Natalie was staying with my uncle when she was…." He diverted his eyes, not finishing the sentence.

"I would love to go with you! I think I could help and it would make me feel useful. And it would give me some time to think about what I want to do with the rest of my life, look at my options in London. And seeing London may bring some of my memory back."

Thinking this proposal over, in deep thought, he finally said, "I'd be a fool to turn down such a generous offer. I would feel better with her killer brought to justice. And it's possible that since you are a woman, you can talk with the ladies and perhaps delve into their secrets. Possibly you could get to know her friends from an outside viewpoint, and potentially uncover new information. I would guess that Natalie confided a lot in her friends."

"Yes, I am good at getting ladies to reveal their secrets, I got that pot roast recipe out of our neighbor, do you remember?"

Ken smiled and said, "Yes, I do remember. Very cunning of you. And it was delicious."

Kate could see the wheels turning as Ken considered how this might work. After a few moments, he offered, "We'll need to come up with a cover for you. Any ideas on who we should say you are?"

"Good question. I guess I could be a long lost relative – someone on the other side of your relations that you just found out about."

Kenneth laughed at the suggestion. "You mean some long lost – kept in the closet - cousin? Some kind of Anastasia scenario – the lady that said she was the Russian princess who survived the murder of her family by the Bolsheviks and was found out to be a fraud. I don't know if I could pull that off. I wouldn't be good at saying such an outlandish story with a straight face."

Kate smiled. "No, I wouldn't think so," she mused.

On a serious note, Kenneth said, looking at her with his thoughtful blue eyes "I've got an idea. We could present you as my fiancée. That would set you up as a future member of my family, people would trust you, and it would be reasonable for me to bring you along to a family wedding. Could you go along with that? I understand if you can't."

What an extraordinary change of events. From possible Nazi to fiancée of a wealthy, handsome, eligible London bachelor in one day. Except the last one wouldn't be real. There was a lot to consider. She would be throwing herself into another situation where she would be leading a double life, although this one would be a much more pleasant scenario. Her thoughts raced. Would jumping into this and seeing London again help her regain her memory, help stop the headaches? Was this a logical next step? Surely this was an excellent opportunity. Besides, she couldn't help getting a little excited about continuing to spend time with Ken and seeing the bright city lights of London.

"Why of course, I can pretend to be your fiancée. That would be a most delightful role."

"It's settled then. And call me Ken, everyone in my family calls me Ken."

"I will call you Ken from now on."

"And this helps me with an issue about a woman who has sights on me romantically."

"Really, do tell."

"A friend of Natalie's, Jolene. I prefer to keep things on a friendship basis, but I'm afraid she wants more."

"Poor Ken, what a burden to be so handsome and irresistible," Kate said with a mischievous smile.

Ken actually blushed. "Don't embarrass me, it's not like that. Anyway, I won't rest until I find out who killed my dear sister. After the killer is locked up, I can move on with my future and life."

"I understand."

"And of course, we'll have to act the part, occasional hugs and kisses and all that. Is that alright with you?"

At that, Kate laughed and stared back at him. He was serious!

Is there any chance he really could have romantic feelings for me?

Ken continued, without looking at her, in a matter of fact tone of voice, "Just to keep up appearances, of course."

"Of course, Ken. Count me in."

"Fantastic. I'll inform my relatives that I will be bringing a surprise guest, and I'll fill in my parents and brother about our plan."

"What about a ring, won't they be suspicious if I don't have an engagement ring on?"

Ken looked at Kate, deep in thought.

Kate hurriedly said, "Of course, I could just say it is being sized, I'm sure that will sound reasonable."

"No, that won't do. We'll take care of that problem as soon as we arrive in London. I know a good jeweler there."

"If you're sure, I don't want to go to extravagant expense, for play-acting. I just thought it might seem suspicious without one."

"Yes, it would indeed. I'm glad you thought of it."

"Well, dear betrothed, let's have lunch, shall we?"

CHAPTER 8

Detective Spencer was having a bad day. First his wife was short with him, complaining about how he was always working too much. Then the dog escaped, and he was late to work after spending an hour chasing the foul creature through the neighborhood of brownstones. Since there was only a collar to grab, it took another 30 minutes to drag the animal home, and the hound was dead-set on resisting every step along the way.

So here he sat at his desk, trying to work on the cold case of Natalie Michaels. The case even made him grumpy. How on earth to make headway on a murder that occurred six years ago? At the time, local police were short-staffed and none of the potential suspects tripped themselves up. No husband with a mistress, no-one holding a grudge against her, the fiancé appeared to be in the clear, no enemies in sight. And all of them upper-class and snobbish, resentful of being spoken to by a detective. Damn, he hated cases like this. And now he was back in the thick of it, all because his supervisor had handed him a packet that supposedly contained new information.

Trouble was it didn't help a bit. It seems a phone call was recently received, which was traced to a public phone booth. The message was a bit garbled, but it sounded like a woman's voice stating that she knew who Natalie Michael's killer was and feared he was going to strike again, then a hang-up. Seeing as since no-one in the area recalled anyone being at that phone booth about the time the call was made, this really wasn't new evidence and didn't provide anything further to follow up on. It very possibly was a crank call. It just put more pressure on him to prevent this supposed second murder from taking place.

Was it this German woman, Katherine Richter? Why would she be involved with a murder, when she was supposedly a dedicated allied spy? Was it Ken or some other member of his family that wanted the case re-opened? Confound it, he'd rather just sit and wait and see what happened. But no, duty called for him to interview suspects again, anyone that knew Natalie Michaels, annoy everyone again, although he felt like it was going to be a complete waste of time.

CHAPTER 9

The next week, Ken and Kate were on their way to London. Sitting for long periods of time was difficult for Kate. The train ride seemed endless and she became more anxious with every mile. Trying to focus on the positive, she moved her thoughts to London and the wedding they would soon be attending. But then she would return to thinking about Ken and her fierce determination to help discover what happened to Natalie. How horrible that she was murdered like that. She sounded like a wonderful person, a dedicated professional with a kind heart.

She went over in her mind again what she and Ken had decided to say about their relationship. The story they invented was this: they met at a dinner being held by James Dawesport, a war buddy of Kenneth's. She would say she was from Newbury, her family had lived there for as long as she could remember. She was working as a secretary for James, who was a local solicitor. He didn't need her help every day, so she had the freedom to take time off when she wanted, such as travel to this wedding. They had been dating for three months, ever since Ken met her at a dinner party.

She already knew a lot about him; it was the fabrications about her life that could trump them up. If anyone asked Ken what her favorite color was, he wouldn't know. At least she knew how to play tennis since she had played with Ken after she had been released from the hospital and he had taught her the rules. She had read all about the current tennis celebrities so that could be an acceptable topic since Ken's circle of friends and family were highly interested in the sport.

Kate knew that everyone was trying to forget about the war and get on with their lives, but it was still going to be in the back of everyone's mind. Her work had obviously been of the utmost secrecy, and playing dual roles meant she had a wealth of knowledge on both German and English politics and policies, and she would have to be careful to keep any information about the war that she remembered, if parts of her memory were to come back, out of her conversations.

"You will never question my authority, right or wrong. You will work as many hours as I need you to. Speed and security will keep Germany leading the world."

She remembered now: her desk facing a window, books and papers haphazardly scattered, her eyes looking down in pretended humbleness as she thought that she would be clenching her teeth every five minutes working for this narcissistic bureaucrat.

"You look lost in thought," Ken said, noticing her keeping still for longer than five minutes. "Are you worried about meeting my family?"

"No, I think I've got them sorted out," She didn't want him to know about the random memories flowing across her thoughts, interrupting the present with haunting visions. "Here goes: your father's name is Albert Michaels, and he is married to Gwendolyn. They are both going to act like they've met me before, we're all cozy friends. You have a much younger brother named Allen, who is 21 years old and attending Oxford, studying medicine. And then there's your cousin, Thomas Eastman, who is getting married to Evelyn. He is the son of your Aunt Margaret, you mother's sister."

"So far so good. And who were Natalie's friends?"

"We will be seeing Andrew, who was Natalie's fiancé and now works at a bank, and her best friend, Jolene, whom you told me about."

"Yes, that's right. Watch out for her, though, she will most likely be very flirtatious with me and might not be too happy that I am showing up engaged and with my fiancée. I think her expectations were to have a romantic relationship with me and clinch it with this wedding. I've run into her a couple times while in London since I've been back and she's indicated as much."

"Thanks for the warning. And then there's Sir Frederick Michaels, your uncle. He is the older brother of your father, at whose house we will be staying. The name of his chauffeur, handy man and valet is Travis. The name of his cook and housekeeper is Anna."

"Excellent, you certainly seem to have a good memory – at least for current things," Ken said, hoping she wouldn't take offence.

She did not. "Your uncle will put us in separate rooms, of course," she added with a twinkle in her eyes.

"Yes, anything else would be scandalous." he said in a teasing way. "And remember, a few romantic gestures to keep up appearances." It almost seemed like a real romance was starting between them. Could it be possible? They say that life imitates art. She turned away, hoping he hadn't noticed her blush slightly at the thought.

"I can tell you take good mental notes, Kate. I wonder what other gems are hidden in your head," he said while facing her and playfully adjusting her collar. "Just remember, it's quite possible someone the family knows or someone at the wedding could have been involved in Natalie's death."

After a moment, he continued, "There's something that I haven't told anyone. Natalie posted a letter to me the day she died, asking me to come to London to talk with her the next time I was scheduled to be in London because she had uncovered something alarming. Something I would never dream of and she wanted to tell me in person. I have been kicking myself for years for not being there when she needed me."

"Ken, you didn't know and it's not your fault. I'm sure you would have tried to get there as soon as you could, when you received the letter. If Natalie thought it was urgent, she would have phoned. She was a reporter, she might have come across something incriminating about someone and they found out and decided to silence her."

"That is a possible scenario," he agreed. "But I still feel responsible. I wish I could have been there for her."

After that somber discussion, Kate became quiet again and retreated to her thoughts. Even though Natalie wrote for the society page, she could just as easily have been covertly covering the upcoming war effort and researching those who lived in England who mistakenly did not think Hitler was dangerous or had such horrible ambitions. Did this lead to her death?

CHAPTER 10

Travis picked them up at the train station in the silver Rolls-Royce. As he opened the door for Kate, she noticed that he was tall and thin with straight chestnut hair that was combed back neatly. Ken had known him for many years, as he had been a mainstay at his uncle's household, doing practically everything for Fred. It seemed as though he and Anna were Fred's companions as well as employees.

The car ride through London did not bring back as many memories for Kate as she had hoped. She tried but couldn't find any familiarity in the endless rows of houses and buildings or in any street names. She held Ken's hand in the back seat and listened as he told her about various historic locations they were passing by.

"It's a bit late to stop by a jewelry shop to buy your ring. We can do that in the morning, is that alright with you?" Ken asked when he remembered that was supposed to be the first stop in London.

"Yes, of course, that will be fine."

During the drive, they went through several areas that had been bombed by the Germans during the Blitz. The ripped-open buildings showing jagged, open mortar walls, with rubbish and pieces of furniture and clothing piled up in front, waiting to be cleaned up and taken away. She turned her head away, preferring to either look at Ken or stare straight ahead, nodding now and then at Ken's comments

"Just around this corner is my uncle's house," Ken finally said. He was a bit tired of keeping the conversation going but didn't want Travis to suspect anything. He could sense Kate's nervousness and had been trying to put her at ease with his casual conversation.

It was a beautiful large Tudor style house, with ivy growing up the walls, solid with a peaked slate roof, decorated posts and carved lions sitting on each side of the wide steps leading to the front door. The architecture was impressive.

Travis pulled their luggage from the back of the car and followed the two as they headed up the stairs. Ken didn't knock. He opened the front door and walked right in, catching Kate's hand as they entered. She gasped at the beauty she saw in the main hall they were standing in, looking at a beautiful crystal chandelier and lovely hard-wood floors.

"Greetings, Ken, it's wonderful to see you again," said an elegant man who was very tall and slender walking toward them. He had grey hair, a rather handsome face and longish nose. He was wearing a black silk dinner jacket, white shirt and black tie. Looking at Kate, he said, "You must be Kate, how lovely to meet you. I'm Ken's uncle, please call me Fred." He held out his hand and smiled at her.

She took it and said "A pleasure to meet you. Ken has said so many good things about you."

"What a surprise, to find our Ken engaged, it took me off-guard since he has never mentioned it before during the many times he has stayed here."

"I didn't want to mention it until she said yes," Ken said with a smile and a chuckle.

"Of course, of course," Fred said, but not very convincingly.

Fred couldn't help noticing that Kate bore a resemblance to Natalie. Her young green eyes were more serious, though, and she was not quite as tall. Fred guessed that perhaps that was one of the reasons Ken was attracted to her. "You're just in time for dinner. Albert and Gwen are here, and Allen is here as well."

Kate took in a deep breath to calm herself. She knew these people wanted to be supportive of her and that Ken's parents and brother were in on the story about their supposed engagement. She smiled at Fred and then followed him and Ken as they walked through the hall and into the large dining room. The room was perfect. The furniture had been polished with loving care. There was a bowl of fresh-cut flowers on the table. Fine crystal and china adorned the table along with a silver tray which would be used for serving the fine cuisine that Anna had prepared.

Albert and Gwen had been looking at one of the paintings on the walnut-paneled wall as they entered. Gwen rushed over to Kate and gave her a hug. "Darling, it's wonderful to see you again. Ken is looking so happy, you must be good for him," she said as she winked at Kate. She was a wide woman, her brownish-grey hair piled nicely on her head with a diamond hairpiece keeping it in place. Her gown was light blue and showed off her full figure. Gwen was certainly friendly and welcoming. Kate was relieved. She knew they would get along fine.

Albert followed with a less effusive hug, and said, "Kate, you look lovely today." He couldn't get over the similarity she had to Natalie, his mind going back briefly to his daughter's laughter and smile. But this woman is very much alive, had saved the life of his son and was going to help him now in trying to solve Natalie's murder. Even if there was a speck of doubt as to whether she worked for MI5, his intuition told him that she was not a deceitful person.

"Allen, come here," he called to the young man who was already sitting at the table. Allen arose and offered his hand to Kate. "So, you're the one everyone is talking about. It's very nice to meet you. However, I don't see how you can put up with my brother!" He said this nonchalantly, but with a smile on his face. "Seriously, though, it's about time he thought about settling down." Kate laughed, happy that Allen was putting her at ease. He looked a lot like Ken, except a younger, more carefree version. The dinner was going to go well, she thought. And she was confident she'd be ready to meet everyone at the wedding, which was taking place the next day.

CHAPTER 11

After dinner, Anna brought Kate to the room she'd be staying in. It was lovelier than she imagined. There was a flowered quilt on the bed, and the tall dresser held a fresh bouquet of flowers. Two tall windows faced west and offered a view of the perfectly landscaped lawn. Kate went to the window and looked out. She turned to see Anna, who had followed her to the window.

"It's beautiful," Kate said.

"Yes, miss, it's a pretty place. There are two washrooms on this floor, one next to your room and the other down the hall. You can hang your clothes in the closet over there or put them in the dresser. It's empty and reserved for guests, although we haven't had any in several years." She added with a warmth to her voice, "And it's nice to have a lady back in the house."

"Thank you, Anna." The woman looked to be about 40, a bit plump, but there was strength in her upper arms and she looked sturdy. She appeared to be supportive of Kate, and perhaps now was a good time to ask her a few questions.

"Have you worked a long time for Sir Fred?"

"Yes, I came to work for him many years ago, not long after he brought this house. It's a big place to be alone in, as you can well imagine," Anna replied, cheerfully walking across the room to adjust a curtain, "Sir Fred is not home much. He travels often and has many business and political dealings. We like it best when he's here, though."

"He's involved in politics?"

"Oh yes, miss, he goes into the heart of the city and is outspoken of his views. His business affairs take him to America at times. The truth is – I believe – that he likes to travel to forget about his dear niece that was murdered in this very house."

"Yes, Ken told me a little about it. It must have been awful. Did you know Natalie well?"

"Yes, she was a darling girl. Sweet as sugar and ambitious. She would have made something of herself. And engaged to be married to a man from a good family. She would have made a beautiful bride. God rest her soul."

"Did you know Andrew well?"

"Not very well, just when he came to visit."

"You said that he came from a good family, but what about him? Did you like him?' Kate worried Anna would feel like she was being interrogated. She smiled at her and said, "I hope you don't mind my questions, Anna, but I just want to know as much as I can about the family and what I'm jumping into."

"Of course, you need to familiarize yourself with the family, you will find they are the best."

"Thank you, I do believe you are right."

"Well, I don't like to gossip," Anna said as she fluffed up the pillows and straightened the quilt on the bed. "But since you will soon be part of the family."

"That's right, and I'm happy to have met you, you have such insight, knowing the family for so long. I promise to keep anything you tell me in confidence."

"Well," Anna said with a sigh, "Mr. Andrew was a little off, if my opinion."

"How so?"

"He was very quiet and would not engage in conversation."

"Perhaps he was just shy."

"No, it wasn't shyness that I observed, more like anger."

"Really? What on earth would he have to feel that way about?"

"I really don't know. Anyway, he joined the forces after Natalie's murder and now the poor dear suffers from shell-shock. He saw horrors that would have been too much for any young man to have to witness."

Anna turned away, apparently not wanting to talk more about Andrew, so Kate changed the subject.

"Tell me about Sir Fred? How did he become knighted?" Kate inquired.

"That was the first great war. He was an officer and a gentleman. He showed leadership and courage in impossible circumstances. It was in 1916 at Vic, near Maricourt, the junction between the English Corps and the French. He and his men held the Front for weeks before receiving reinforcements. Quite the hero, but you would never know it, he doesn't put on airs. Humility is a family trait, as you no doubt will find out."

Kate smiled and said, "Yes, I believe I already have."

"I'm certain you will be very happy to be part of this family, miss, and we look forward to getting to know you."

Anna looked down at Kate's hand to see if she had a ring on.

Kate noticed and quickly said, "Ken wanted to wait until we got to London to buy me a ring. We are going to do that tomorrow, before the wedding."

"How lovely, there are some fine jewelers in London."

"What about you, Anna? Do you have a family?"

"My dear Harold was an officer in the infantry and lost his life in the war, during the Battle of the Bulge. I miss him terribly. We thought he would be back. He was the finest of men."

Kate could tell by Anna's change in demeanor that she was still grieving for him. "I am so sorry, Anna. I'm sure he was a fine man and you have suffered a terrible loss."

"Thank you." She composed herself and continued, "I also have a daughter, Miranda, she is seventeen. You will probably meet her, she comes around from time to time to help me with the garden, laundry, and such."

"I'll be delighted to meet her, I'm sure."

"Best to focus on the positive, I've learned," Anna looked at Kate with growing affection. It wasn't every woman who cared about staff. It was nice to talk to someone, in her position she was often quite lonely. Changing the subject to something more pleasant, she added, "The family will soon be celebrating a joyous occasion – the wedding of two lovely young people. And who would have guessed that Ken would be bringing along a lovely fiancée as yourself. He didn't tell us he was engaged." She smiled at Kate and said, "You seem a thoughtful woman and I think you'll be a good match for Ken. Everyone will be delighted and surprised."

Not everyone, thought Kate thinking about Jolene and her designs on Ken. She knew there was at least one woman that would be very disappointed.

"Ken tells me you are a marvelous cook and Sir Fred is lucky to have found you."

"Well, isn't that kind of Ken. I do make every effort to set a good table." With mention of her duties, Anna's thoughts turned to her responsibilities and she walked to the door, only to hesitate there and turn toward Kate.

"I am so glad that Ken has brought a fiancée with him. We're all hoping life will get on as normal now that the war in Europe is over."

As Kate bent over her case and lifted it on the bed, she could feel Anna eyeing her.

"I had a feeling Ken was up to something, never staying long when he came to London, always wanting to get back to the country without delay, even though he never was partial to his cottage before, to that extent. Now I see it was you he was anxious to get back to." Anna said this with a smile and a giggle.

Kate smiled back in return as she opened her case and started taking out her clothes.

"Good night, dear" Anna said as she walked through the door.

"Good night, Anna, and thank you for your hospitality."

CHAPTER 12

Evelyn's wedding gown was beautiful. The solid white silk dress was covered with intricately woven beaded flowers streaming down from her shoulders to her waist. It had been her mother's and she was honored to be able to wear it. Her hourglass figure was accentuated by the floor-length flowing skirt that flared from her tiny waistline, with a long train that two very young girls were holding up, trailing behind her as she walked up the aisle. Her father gently held her upper arm as the two headed toward the altar.

Kate was in awe, staring at the lovely bride and Thomas, her husband-to-be, who stood there patiently, his eyes only on Evelyn as she drew closer and closer. Kate briefly considered what it would feel like walking in those shoes, with Ken standing there waiting for her. But that was nonsense. She had no clue how he felt about her, and if he was even the kind of man who wanted to be married. Perhaps he was a confirmed bachelor, like his uncle Fred.

Kate's thoughts reverted back to the events before the ceremony began. They had risen early to stop at Ken's favorite jewelry shop, where Kate picked out a sparkling 1.2 caret, round cut diamond engagement ring. It took Kate's breath away as she put it on her left hand.

"Looks pretty convincing," Ken said with a laugh, looking her straight in the eyes. The two connected for a brief, poignant moment, then Ken took her arm and they returned to the car, rather in a hurry, heading off to the church where the wedding was to be held. It turned out Ken had a small red MG sports car that he kept in London for transportation when he was there.

They actually arrived early, not wanting to worry about traffic or any circumstance that could cause them to be late. Ken believed in being prompt, which was one of his personality traits that Kate found endearing.

There had been introductions as she and Ken entered the walled gardens outside of the church. Jolene stood out in her mind as being the most difficult woman she had met so far. She was quite beautiful with dark brown hair and long eyelashes over bright expressive brown eyes. She knew that she caught every man's eye when she walked into a room. She wore extensive makeup, bright red lipstick, and a glistening pale green gown that was a bit more revealing than would be expected at a wedding in a conservative church. A white stole was draped loosely over her shoulders. It was obvious to Kate that Jolene intentionally dressed that way in order to gain attention.

Ken introduced them briefly as they walked by. Kate could tell Jolene was infatuated with him by the way she looked at him and totally ignored her, not even an ounce of acknowledgement. Did Ken notice that?

He left her alone for a moment while he chatted with an old friend.

"So you're the infamous woman who has somehow charmed our dear Ken," Jolene said, appearing suddenly, with a small smile that she reserved for her social inferiors and in a tone that was not quite sincere. "And where did you say you met him?"

"We met in Newbury, I work for one of his friends.

"How lovely. I've known Ken for many years, and I'm surprised he would fall for someone so quickly. I'm very curious. How did you manage to bewitch him? Tell me, how long have you been engaged?"

Kate was astonished this woman could be so blunt. "It has been a bit of a whirlwind romance. We've only been engaged for a few weeks. I'm honored that he decided to bring me to London to meet his family and attend this wedding," she answered with as much lightness as she could muster, not-so-subtly looking down at the brilliant diamond ring on her left hand. "It's very nice to meet you."

"You as well," Jolene said with a raised eyebrow and a skeptical look as she glanced down at Kate's hand, turned her back on Kate and walked toward a group of others. Kate sighed. She hadn't intended to get off on the wrong foot with the woman who had been Natalie's best friend. But she couldn't help responding in kind.

She wasn't alone for more than a minute when a gentleman came up to her. He was an attractive man in a tailored tux with a confident air about him. He seemed friendly and unusually interested in her.

What now? Kate thought.

"Hello Kate, I'm Dexter Flynn," the man said, pulling her hand toward him and taking a few extra moments when kissing it, checking out her engagement ring. He let go of her hand and looked her in the eyes. "I understand you are Ken's latest flame."

"If you want to call me that, yes. Actually, I'm his fiancée. How did you know my name?"

"I try to know as much as I can about everyone, it's my job. I work for the *Times* as a reporter."

"That's right, Ken mentioned you would be here. You knew Natalie as well?"

"I did, very well, she was a lovely woman and I miss her terribly. We all do. You're a breath of fresh air, my dear. I'm very glad Ken has found someone reasonable to spend his time with."

This was a veiled compliment and Kate was pleased. "We met a few months ago at a dinner party. I live in Newbury."

"You don't say. I've been there. Do you know Russell Jones, the manager at Essex bank? He's an old friend."

"No, I bank elsewhere."

"Have you always lived in Newbury?"

Just then Ken returned to her side. "Dexter, nice to see you," he said, rescuing her from having to answer more questions. "Do you think it's going to rain this afternoon?"

"There's a 75% chance, according to the *Times* weather report." Dexter then bowed his head slightly at Kate, and headed toward the church doors.

"Dexter's a nice chap, but he can be a bit overly inquisitive. I hope he wasn't giving you a hard time," Ken said to Kate, putting his arm around her.

What a nice feeling, Ken being so close to her. "Nothing I couldn't handle," she answered, just wanting Ken to continue holding her, enjoying his warmth.

"I know you'll be fine."

Another man, a bit stiff with a serious manner and graying hair, came up to them. Ken took his arm away from Kate and held out his hand in greeting.

"Franklin, so nice to see you. How are you?" The two shook hands. "I would like to introduce you to Kate, my fiancée." Turning toward Kate, he added "Franklin is our financial advisor and does the accounting for my parents and Uncle Fred."

"A pleasure to meet you, Franklin," Kate said, offering her hand as well. Franklin was clearly surprised at the announcement that Ken was engaged and shook her hand rather limply.

"So, you like to work with numbers?" Kate said.

"Yes, they consume me, they are my best friends. Money makes the world go around in more ways than you can imagine," he said abruptly and stiffly turned toward another couple nearby.

That was weird, thought Kate.

"Franklin can be awkward at times but he's a good person," Ken said quietly to her.

Kate took in the information and noticed that everyone, with the exception of Jolene, seemed very nice but somehow in her thoughts she knew that even the most innocent-seeming person could be guilty of the most horrible things, especially if they became desperate.

"Yes, I'm sure he's a good person," she had responded.

Ken gently pulled her arm and said, "There are two important people you must meet." He walked along with her, guiding her toward a sidewalk branching off to the side of the building. It ended at an arbor covered in ivy, with a bench on which Kate saw a young man sitting with an older man. The two of them looked alike and she thought they might be father and son. The older man stood up and extended his hand to Ken.

"Greetings Ken, it's a blessing to see you again. At least in better circumstances than the last time."

Kate presumed that he was referring to Natalie's funeral. Kate noticed a slight hint of – could it be malice, or unhappiness – in his eyes when he looked at Ken. Why on earth would he be upset with Ken? She thought she must be imagining things.

The man turned to her. "And this must be Kate. Nice to meet you, young lady, he said, taking her hand. He held it for a few seconds longer than expected, making her feel a bit uncomfortable.

"I'm George Cresswell, and this young man is my son, Andrew," he said. "Andrew, please stand up, remember your manners."

"Yes, pleased to meet you," Andrew said in a monotone voice as he reluctantly arose and took her hand and then quickly let go. His appearance was a bit morose and sullen. His face was long and thin, he had light hair and full lips that turned down at the edges. He was also tall and thin. Kate wondered if he was always glum like this or if this occasion brought back painful memories of Natalie's death and the wedding they were planning to have. Ken had told her that Natalie's murder had devastated him. Anna had said he was troubled when he returned from the war. Kate could see how he would be handsome if his spirits were brighter.

"Andrew was among the many fighting in France during the war," Ken explained. "We're grateful he came back safely."

So, this was the man that Natalie was to marry. He must have been very different before he joined up, and Kate recognized the symptoms of shell-shock. She saw much of it when she was in the hospital. How horrible to lose the woman he was going to marry and then fight in the bloody war on top of it. Life was so unfair.

It had started out as a lovely summer day, surely a good sign for the couple getting married. But clouds were starting to form and the sky darkened a bit as the organ music began inside the church.

The sound of the choir singing a hymn brought her back to the present. The church was full, the flowers were beautiful, but the ceremony was long and tedious. When the newly-married couple finally gave each other a short kiss, signaling the end of the ceremony, everyone breathed a sigh of relief.

It took a while to exit through the throngs of people, all of whom Ken seemed to know and had to greet. Some he introduced Kate to, some he did not. She glided through it all, trying to note everyone she met, looking for nervousness or guilt but finding none. How could any of these people have harmed Natalie?

CHAPTER 13

The wedding reception, which followed the church ceremony, was held at the Ness Hotel. Ken dropped Kate and Fred off near the front entryway, while he went to park the car. As Kate stepped onto the curb, she looked back at the car and noticed a man with a red bow tie standing several feet away. He was staring at her intently. As she looked at him, wondering what on earth he wanted, he slipped into a group of people and disappeared. How strange, she thought, then promptly forgot about him as she entered the hotel and followed the crowd, Fred at her side, to the brightly-decorated dining room.

Ken arrived a few minutes later. The dinner was delightful and champagne flowed. Although the newlyweds were gracious and enjoying themselves, Kate guessed they were anxious to get on with their honeymoon, which was to take place in Scotland, where the bride's family owned an estate. Scanning the guests, Kate noticed that Andrew sat at a table with his family but did not seem to socialize much.

Another person to whom Kate was introduced was Edward Aylesworth, a Member of Parliament who was apparently a good friend of the Michaels family. He held out his hand to Kate and she noticed he had cold-as-steel grey-blue eyes. She looked in them directly, but they revealed nothing, neither warmth nor disdain. She hoped he would approve of her as Ken's fiancée. It was hard to smile at everyone and act interested. MP Aylesworth's wife, Julia, was especially elegant. Kate thought she looked like a film star.

In addition to the friends and family Kate had met before the wedding, she was introduced to another of Ken's cousins, Amanda. With a warm and friendly demeanor, Amanda was a

graceful woman who helped put Kate at ease. Her blonde hair was
perfectly styled in a fashionable chin-length cut and she wore an
elegant blue beaded dress. She was seated next to Ken and Kate
and they engaged in small talk, discussing the harmonious
ceremony and what a smart couple the bride and groom made. Ken
seemed to have a high regard for his cousin and eventually the two
brought up some of their childhood memories, sharing laughter
and anecdotes. Amanda mentioned that her parents were abroad
but had sent along their congratulations to the bride and groom.

Then a man and woman arrived that Kate had noticed at the
ceremony but had not been introduced to. When they came to the
table, Kate was surprised to see Amanda's mood drastically
change. Amanda, Kate noticed, held her champagne glass in her
manicured fingers so tight it looked like it might break in her
hand. They were introduced to Kate as Mr. and Mrs. Patel and
their son, Rajimin, who appeared at their side.

Of Indian descent, Mrs. Patel was dressed in a bright red and
gold silk sari, while her husband and son wore contemporary
English suits. Rajimin was dark-skinned and handsome, with a
surprisingly humble air about him. "Call me Raj" he said to Kate
as he took her hand and kissed it lightly. Raj nodded to Amanda
and smiled but Amanda only looked up at him and his parents
briefly without any kind words of acknowledgement.

While the Patels sat at another table, Amanda's mood was
noticeably distant the rest of the dinner, and she avoided even
looking at the Patel family. When she left for the powder room,
Kate looked at Ken. As if to answer the question in her eyes, Ken
very quietly informed her that Amanda had once had a romantic
liaison with Rajimin. "As it turned out, they could not get married
because Raj was already betrothed, an arranged marriage by his
family."

"Really, how medieval. That still happens in this day and age?"

"Oh yes. I imagine it will happen well into the next century, the
tradition is so ingrained in their culture."

"Really?"

"I've heard that the divorce rate is much smaller in arranged marriages than in the general married population."

Kate laughed, "I prefer to believe one should have the freedom to make one's own mistakes."

"I feel the same way."

"So, what happened? Did Raj ever marry the woman he was betrothed to?"

"No, not yet, with the war and everything. But the engagement is still on I believe. As you can see, Amanda is very bitter about the whole situation."

"I would imagine so."

The rest of the evening was uneventful. Kate was relieved when the dinner was over and everyone went outside to wish the bride and groom adieu as they got into their car to head out for their honeymoon.

Dancing began and the party continued. Kate was impressed at how well Ken danced and everyone had a good time. They waltzed, tangoed, fox-trotted all the way until the stroke of midnight, when Ken and Kate then said their goodbyes. Travis had driven Fred to the church so he had no transportation home, but he told Ken to go ahead and leave without him and he would get a ride later from some friends. Kate made a point of taking Andrew's hand and telling him it was a pleasure to meet him. She also wanted to tell Amanda goodbye but couldn't find her.

Ultimately, Kate felt overwhelmed, responding to the large number of people seemingly everywhere, and the extensive socialization she had not experienced before. Smiling constantly at everyone and playing the outsider fiancée was taking its toll on her. Ken brought the car around and got out to open the door for Kate. As she got into the car, she collapsed into her seat and closed her eyes. Ken got back in the driver's seat and pulled out into the street.

"Kate, you're a trooper. Thanks for being so calm and collected through all this." He looked at her when she didn't respond and realized she had fallen asleep.

CHAPTER 14

After most of the people left the party, George and Elaine Cresswell moved to a booth in the back of the bar area of the hotel. MP Edward and Julia Aylesworth joined them for a quiet conversation. They all wanted to get away from the band and the dancing. The men enjoyed cigars and whiskies.

"What did you think of Ken's intended? That was certainly a surprise," George commented.

"It certainly was, but I think she's a darling," Elaine answered.

"Does anyone know where's she's from?" Edward asked.

"He met her in the country, he has a cottage there, in Newbury," Elaine answered again.

"That explains why he has spent so much time there, I often wondered what he was up to." George took a swallow of his drink.

The women continued the conversation.

"Have they set a date?" Julia asked.

"No, not yet. I think Ken just proposed within the last few days. Odd, to bring her to a family event at the spur of the moment and when no-one was expecting it. I guess he thought it would be fun to surprise everyone."

"Well, he has always been full of surprises."

"She has a strong resemblance to Natalie."

There were a few moments of silence. Julia observed her companions carefully, studying their faces, as she sipped her drink.

Then George spoke, "Well, hopefully, after Ken is married, he will come to live in London and concentrate on his business affairs!"

CHAPTER 15

The day after the wedding, everyone slept in late. The partying had gone on past midnight and Fred danced until the end. He was one of the last to leave the reception and didn't come out of his room until noon.

Kate wandered down to the dining room around 10 o'clock and was pleased to see Ken sitting alone at the massive table, almost dwarfed by the high ceilings, dark walls and family portraits.

He turned and looked at her, an inquiring look in his eyes. "After we eat, would you be interested in going to the constabulary and meeting with the inspector who originally investigated Natalie's murder?"

"Ken, you are on top of it, as usual. Yes, I'd love to go, splendid idea."

Ken drove to the constabulary, parking the car nearby. The department was a busy place, with uniformed officers heading here and there, chairs filled with worried men and women waiting their turns to file complaints. Typewriters were clacking, voices raised and hushed, almost in a constant hum. Ken had the forethought to call Inspector Madison to set an appointment, so their wait was brief.

"Greetings, Mr. Michaels and Miss Richter," Inspector Madison said as Ken and Kate entered his office. The inspector had brown unkept hair and wore a white shirt with the sleeves rolled up and a black tie. The room was full of shelves with books and papers scattered everywhere. Kate wondered how he found anything in the apparent mess. "Please sit down here," he said as he motioned them to a dusty metal table with two rickety-looking chairs across from his desk.

They sat down and were handed a thick manila folder that was ruffled and dusty. "Here's the file you requested. Hope it helps you. If you don't mind, I'm going to continue working while you look at it, I can't let you take it anywhere." He immediately began peering through his thick glasses at one of the stacks of papers on his desk and ignored the two.

Ken and Kate read every sheet in the folder, each scanning the details, looking for anything the police may have missed, anything that would help them figure out who the perpetrator was.

The detectives had come to a dead end in their search for the killer. They had interviewed Natalie's friends, family, co-workers, and most of them had solid alibis for the timeframe in which she was strangled. The reports said that her jewelry was still in her room, money was still in her purse, so they were certain it wasn't a robbery. However, her journal was missing, and there were no papers on her desk or in her typewriter. Police suspected she had been killed deliberately, but there were no clues to be found. It was just one of many unsolved murders that year in London and with war being declared and a shortage of staff, they were limited in how far they could pursue the case.

When Ken finally closed up the folder and stood up, Madison said, "I'm sorry we weren't able to solve this one. Never feel good when we can't close things up tight."

Ken gave Kate an exasperated look and said to Madison, "Thank you very much, sir. We appreciate your efforts and letting us see the file. We are playing sleuths ourselves, and maybe we'll be able to find the killer."

"Scotland Yard's best is working on it. Detective Spencer is noted for his persistence, but you never know. Please keep me informed if you have new information on the case."

"Will do, sir," Ken responded.

The pair headed out into the busy street toward where the car was parked. They walked slowly, each absorbed in their own thoughts, very quiet. Kate's mind was swirling as she tried to picture the people she'd met who were close enough to Natalie to be worried about what she had in her journal or her papers. It must have been someone she knew, which means it quite possibly was someone they were currently attending parties with.

"That wasn't very productive," she mused. "I was thinking that I would like to go to the library tomorrow and look up articles that were in the newspaper at the time of the crime. Maybe I could find out something there that the inspectors have missed."

"Yes, that would be a splendid idea. I'm playing tennis with Andrew tomorrow. I know he enjoys the game and I think it will do him a world of good, get his mind off of things."

"I couldn't agree more."

Ken then told her he would be out the rest of the day in order to take care of some business interests. Kate agreed that he should attend to his business and followed with a comment on needing some time to relax. She spent the rest of the day reading and thinking, retiring early to her room after barely touching her dinner. The last few days had been the most sociable she'd had in her life, at least as much as she could remember of it, and she found it extremely tiring dealing with so many people. She easily fell asleep without even trying.

CHAPTER 16

The next morning Kate followed up on her idea to visit the library to find articles about Natalie's murder in the newspapers around the time when she was killed.

The plan was for her to meet Ken, Andrew and Fred for lunch at Fred's favorite tavern, after Ken's tennis match with Andrew and her research quest. Following their light breakfast and tea, Ken and Kate went for a short walk. It was nice to feel the fresh cool air, if only for a few moments. Ken wished her good luck in her search, and she wished him a challenging game. Before he left, Ken gave Kate a kiss on the cheek in front of Fred and his staff to keep up appearances.

Travis drove Kate to the library and she instructed him to come back in two hours. She figured that would be enough time for her investigations and, if she had extra time, she could always entertain herself wandering around the library. After walking up the stairs toward the entrance, she could sense someone behind her. Reaching for the door handle, a warm hand gently enveloped hers and with a start she turned to look over her shoulder to see Dexter Flynn.

"Fancy meeting you here," he said as they faced each other at the entrance.

"Indeed. Good morning Mr. Flynn."

"What brings you here?"

"I want to look for old newspaper articles about the murder of Natalie Michaels. Why are you here?"

"I really can't say. It has to do with research on a piece that I'm writing for the *Times.*"

"Yes, that's right. I remember you are an investigative reporter and, if I remember right, you are very well received, dare I say, some of your pieces have won worldwide accolades."

"Oh, you've heard of me. Thank you for the compliment and acknowledging my work." He smiled, surprised that she was aware of him.

Kate nodded. "Now that the war in Europe is over, what will you be writing about?"

"The war in Europe doesn't seem to be over, or never will be, for some, I'm afraid. Take Andrew for example. That poor fellow will never be the same. Shell-shock. We saw it in the Great War and we see it again now."

"Yes, Ken tells me his parents say he has terrible flash-back nightmares every night. I feel for him. I only wish I could do something to help."

"I noticed you were kind to him at the reception."

"It's the very least I could do."

"He'll come out of it with time but he'll probably never be exactly the same as he was before. None of us will probably be exactly the same as we were before."

"I guess not. Tell me, are you covering the still raging war in the Pacific?"

"I am covering the events there but I'm working on a special project as well."

Dexter put his hand on Kate's shoulder and opened the door for them to walk in. "If you'll follow me, I'll show you where you can find the articles you're looking for."

"That would be very kind of you, thank you."

They walked along a maze of hallways until Dexter stopped in front of one of the doors. Turning the handle, he motioned her inside. It was a dusty room with countless rows of newspapers. Kate sat down at a long table and asked Dexter if he could spare a minute since she wanted to talk to him. He sat down opposite her at the table.

"May I ask you something," Kate said.

He smiled. "Yes, how may I be of service?"

"Who do you think might have had reason to murder Natalie Michaels?"

She had hoped to see some sign of guilt or secret knowledge but saw only sorrow in his eyes.

"I have no idea."

"Surely you must have some suspicions. You said she was a friend and colleague. You must have thought about it before now."

He looked deep in thought and finally spoke. "She wrote for the society column. Maybe she found out something embarrassing about someone. That is what I have always thought."

Kate was aghast. "Would someone really murder to protect their reputation?"

"Yes, I believe they would. You must not know the people you are associating with, my dear."

"I guess they are a little out of my league."

"Does Ken's family mind?"

"Mind what?"

"That you are not from their class, so to speak, a commoner, someone with humble beginnings...."

"Yes, I get it. These aren't feudal times, Mr. Flynn."

"Whatever you say," Dexter said, staring at her intently.

"And I'm not an innocent little girl, I just haven't spent a lot of time with people who commit murder." After these words came out of her mouth, she realized this was an absolute lie, as she must have lived daily with murderers at her post in Germany. She hoped her face didn't give her away.

Kate couldn't be bothered with this class discussion and was getting slightly annoyed. She had other things to occupy her mind. But there was a gem in what he had said. Dexter's comments shed light on many more suspects and not just the immediate friends and family that she had met. Now she wanted to examine all the articles that Natalie had written prior to her demise.

As if reading her mind, he offered, "Here, I'll show you where to find all articles from that time period. Not only about her murder but the paper that she was working for and articles that she had written. Will that help?"

"Yes, that will help immensely, and I won't take up any more of your time. Thank you very much."

"You are welcome."

They parted on excellent terms, Dexter expressing his desire to see her again while she was in London, leaving to pursue his own reasons for his library visit.

Kate noticed that he never mentioned anything about Ken and that he seemed to be a bit flirtatious with her. She hoped that his investigative instincts were not leading him to believe that Ken and Kate were not the engaged couple that they were claiming to be.

Looking through articles from the days after Natalie's murder, she did not glean much more than what she and Ken had learned from the police file the day before. She did, however, come across something that caught her attention. It was an interview with one of the first constables on the scene who had interviewed Sir Frederick Michaels.

According to the article, the astute policeman asked about Natalie's engagement ring, noting that she was engaged to be married. Frederick Michaels acknowledged that Natalie's engagement ring was missing. That was news! There was no mention of this in the file and it could be very important. The file said that all her jewelry had been accounted for. Why hadn't Fred mentioned it in the official statement he had given later to the police?

Although, Kate thought, this could throw suspicion on Jolene. Kate had heard Jolene had been dating Andrew before he met Natalie. Someone, she was not sure who, had said Jolene accused Natalie of stealing Andrew away from her. But how could she and Jolene have remained friends after that? Was Jolene the kind of person who was double-sided, pretending to be Natalie's friend but secretly hating her? Could jealousy have led to murder? Jealousy is a powerful emotion.

Now the question was whether or not she should tell Ken about this. No, it didn't seem appropriate for her to run to Ken with this information like some excited rival for his attentions. Not yet, not until she had a chance to talk to Fred about it. Maybe the ring had finally turned up and that's why he never mentioned it in his official statement. The alternative would be that he was protecting someone, possibly Jolene. She hoped he would be honest with her when she confronted him about it.

Kate then looked at the paper for which Natalie wrote the society pages but could not find any articles that would be worth killing for. Most of the news clips were about fashion and very complimentary towards the people Natalie mentioned. What a lovely gown Miss So-and-So had on at the ball . . . Or notice the stunning necklace on Mrs. Whomever . . .

It was closing in on her allotted two hours and she knew Travis would soon be waiting for her return. Standing up, she thought she might try to find Dexter, if he was still at the library, to tell him goodbye. Retracing the route through the hallways, she found him as she looked through a glass door in a small room, in deep discussion with another gentleman. Kate was surprised to see that it was the man with the red bow tie she had noticed watching her as she got out of the car to attend the wedding reception. He seemed to stare at her at that time and was taking special notice of her now as she peered through the window. She waved to Dexter from the window. He glanced up, smiled at her, and waved back. He did not, however, open the door and allow her to meet this mysterious man.

Travis was waiting for Kate in the Rolls. He got out and opened the door for her, then returned to the driver seat. He pulled away from the curb and soon she was at the tavern, just in time for lunch.

Ken, Andrew and Fred were seated at a table when Kate arrived. They had already been served drinks. All three rose as Ken pulled out a chair for Kate. She nodded to Ken and Fred and touched Andrew's shoulder. "Good afternoon Andrew, how are you today?"

"Fine, thank you. However, Ken showed no mercy at tennis. He beat me soundly," Andrew said with more enthusiasm than he had shown in the last few days.

Perhaps he had become anxious with the crowds at the wedding. He seemed a lot more relaxed and friendly than previously and Kate was glad to see it.

"Well, he can be like that," Kate said with a smile. "He is quite competitive."

Fred and Andrew started talking about the latest trends in cigars and wine, and Ken turned to her.

"Did you find out anything at the library?" he asked quietly out of earshot of the other two.

"Nothing we hadn't learned from our visit to the constabulary yesterday." Kate did not look Ken in the eye when she spoke, hoping he couldn't tell she was not being completely honest. Whatever lies she may have told in her previous life, she could not look Ken in the eye and not be completely truthful with him.

Just then the waiter came over and asked Kate if she wanted something to drink.

"A lemonade, please."

Fred took a sip of his drink and spoke to Kate and Ken. "Are you two conspiring? I don't feel comfortable about you two trying to investigate Natalie's murder. It is a matter that is best left to the police. If it is possible to solve it at all. It's a cold case and so much has happened since. I have assisted the police in any way that I can. The murder was committed at my house and I feel somewhat responsible. I still feel bad that I hadn't been home that night."

Kate didn't think it an appropriate time to ask Fred about the ring. Her plan was to talk to him later, when she had a chance to see him alone. But neither she nor Ken responded to his comments, both not wanting to start an argument and determined to continue their sleuthing. They looked down and did not respond.

Fortunately, the waiter came by to take their order and the rest of the lunch was spent in light conversation, mostly about sporting events and their shared love of tennis.

After finishing their meals, the group went to Fred's house to play cards and relax for the rest of the afternoon and evening. Nothing more was said about their sleuthing.

Lost Secrets

CHAPTER 17

Jolene awoke the day after the wedding gasping for air. She'd had a nightmare she was being choked to death. How awful, she thought, when she realized that was exactly how Natalie had died. It took her at least twenty minutes to come around to reality and relax enough to get up. It wasn't the first time she'd been plagued by bad dreams.

The last six years had been difficult. She was on a date with Andrew when he met Natalie, her best friend, at a party. He never gave her a second look after that, only seemed to want to be with Natalie. Natalie apologized if she had interfered in a budding relationship and Jolene should have forgiven her, since they'd only been out once. But it wasn't fair, Andrew was the one she'd had her eye on for months, and she'd really fallen for him. Natalie always was the more interesting one of the two friends. They had grown up together, and she never mentioned it, but she always felt like she was second best. Like the not-as-cute little sister that people ignored. After Natalie's death she began learning how to appear more interesting and exciting. She decided to dress in a revealing manner showing off her figure, just because she could do so and discovered that the men loved it.

Most men anyway. After Natalie died, and Andrew was off limits, she turned her radar toward Ken Michaels. She'd known him all her life as well. But he was really withdrawn after Natalie was gone and took off to fight the Germans, joining the RAF. Then Andrew left as well and she felt quite alone. There was no-one to be close to anymore, no-one to share her thoughts with.

She had run into Ken in front of the bank building one day, a few months ago, in May.

"My goodness, could that possibly be my dear friend Ken?" she had asked in a flirtatious manner.

"It is. And you have changed quite a bit, Jolene, since I've last seen you."

"I heard you were a stellar pilot and won awards and honors during the war. It was hard staying in London, especially during the blitz. I volunteered with the Red Cross for a while."

"Really. I'm impressed that you would volunteer your time to help."

"I know of a wonderful pub where we could have a nice lunch," she offered, not wanting to get into details about the week she'd spent trying to work, which didn't suit her at all so she hadn't stayed.

"Sorry, I'm very busy, but maybe next time I'm in London. I still have your phone number." With that he had taken his leave and headed down the block at a quick pace.

Damn, she blew her chance. Was she too forward? She was determined to forget it and forgive herself for it, but it was difficult. She only wanted to get to know more about Ken. It was high time she was married, and he was the best potential candidate.

A few weeks later, she ran into Ken again, at a popular nightclub and had a chance to talk with him. Again, he was friendly but aloof to her charms.

"You said you would call the next time you came to London."

"I'm sorry, I haven't had a chance to call. I only come to London for business and my time here is very limited." Then he said in a light-hearted tone of voice, "But I'm here now and so are you. It is very nice to see you and you look wonderful. Would you like to dance?"

They enjoyed a popular jitter-bug and then a drink together afterward. He was sociable but seemed blind to her flirtations. She was surprised to find out that he was living in the country and he did not elaborate on why or what he was doing there. All his business dealings were in London. Why wouldn't he live here? He left the nightclub abruptly after he finished his drink with a vague promise to keep in touch.

And then the next time she saw him, there was this dreadful surprise at the wedding. No-one had told her Ken was engaged. How could he do that to her? This woman was pretty, she had to admit, but didn't talk much and didn't seem to care about the latest fashions. It was surprising that she had a look of Natalie about her. Every time she looked over at this woman and Ken, they were smiling at each other, looking happy. Very distressing.

Ken was attentive when she threw on the charm, but he was still going back to Sir Fred's house with this Kate person. And he was going to marry her? Seemed a bit suspicious that nothing had been said about a date and he hadn't mentioned anything the times she saw him in London. It seemed all very curious and rushed into. She would do her best to get him to change his mind and see that she was the better catch and a more suitable wife for a man in his position.

Lost Secrets

CHAPTER 18

A few days went by, peaceful, lovely days. Another after-wedding party was to be held at the Ness Hotel that weekend. Kate had not found the perfect moment to approach Fred about the missing ring and hadn't talked to Ken about it. It was a beautiful morning, so Fred and Ken had gone to play golf. Kate sat down at the dining room table, picked up the morning newspaper and began to read it. A young girl came out of the kitchen with a tray that held a pot of tea and a cup.

She smiled and said, "Good morning." She looked about seventeen. Her bright eyes and warm skin were attractive but Kate noticed her hair was not styled and she wore a tattered dress.

"You must be Miranda, Anna's daughter. I am pleased to meet you!"

Miranda nodded. "I am happy to meet you, miss. What would you like for breakfast? I'll tell my mum."

"Just toast and jam this morning, we had a late dinner."

Miranda walked back into the kitchen. A few moments later, Anna came into the room with toasted fresh bread and homemade jam that she served to Kate.

"Thank you, Anna. I just met your daughter, what a doll. Will she be helping you today?"

"Yes, she's out of school and helps me from time to time."

"How nice."

"She's not too happy right now and I'm trying to keep her busy, keep her mind off of things."

"Why, what's wrong?"

"She has a slight crush on the boy that works at the motor repair garage, Jeremy. There is a youth dance this weekend at our church and she has been hoping he would ask her to it. So far, no luck."

"She must be very disappointed."

After Kate finished her toast and jam, she took her plate into the kitchen. Anna was cleaning green beans from the garden to prepare for the evening meal. Miranda was out in the garden.

"Anna, would it be okay if I talked to Miranda, took her to my room? I think I have some clothes that would fit her, I brought them with me but they are a little too small for me."

Anna shrugged her shoulders. "Sure."

Kate went out to the garden and soon Miranda was in Kate's room.

"First of all, let's move your hair out of your pretty face," Kate said as she brought Miranda's hair back and into a pony tail. "Perhaps a little make-up."

A cute, cotton dress, white with small flowers, fit Miranda well, to Kate's surprise. After the make-over, they walked down stairs and into the kitchen. Anna gasped when she saw her daughter. "You look lovely!"

The pair then went into the garage where Travis was washing the Rolls.

"Travis, I could hear a strange noise in the car the last time I rode in it." Kate remarked.

"What? Travis looked at them, surprised to see Miranda with lipstick on.

"I think you should take it to the motor repair garage."

Travis had a confused look on his face for a moment, but then he smiled, looked at them both, and then quickly realized exactly what Kate was up to.

"Yes, I think I will take it there. I heard the noise too."

"Perhaps you might take Miranda with you," she said with a twinkle in her eye.

"I believe I will."

"Thank you, Travis."

CHAPTER 19

Saturday rolled around and Ken and Fred were getting ready for another party at the Ness Hotel. Ken and Kate had gone shopping earlier in the day to buy new clothes to wear.

Travis brought the Rolls around to the front and left it running, as Ken was planning to drive. As they were getting in the car, Anna came outside to tell them goodbye.

"Do you have any plans this evening?" Kate asked. "Or does Miranda?"

Anna grinned. "Now that you mention it, Miranda is going to her first teen dance."

"Alone?"

"No, she has a date. You can probably guess with whom." She winked at Kate.

Kate smiled and closed the car door.

Ken asked, "What is that about?"

"Women business."

They sped off in the direction of the hotel.

The party was quite the affair with dinner, dancing and champagne, not to mention martinis and fine wine. Kate wore a lovely dark blue silk gown which accented her delicate features. Ken looked dashing in his black dinner jacket with a blue bow tie which matched Kate's gown. The dining room was elegant and pristine with white linen tablecloths and napkins, with each table adorned with a sparkling crystal centerpiece designed in the various geometrical shapes, quite an extravagance, Kate thought.

Ken and Kate sat at a table with Ken's parents, his brother Allen, Fred, and Dexter Flynn. Kate again noticed the official-looking man in his mid-forties with the red bow tie whom she had seen at the reception and again at the library. He was several tables away and seemed to be taking particular note of them. Kate could think of no reason why he would be observing her so she granted him only a curious glance. She didn't feel quite brave enough to confront him. Then, when he disappeared, she thought no more about it.

Anyway, Kate had her hands full with Dexter and the interest he seemed to have in her. The other members of the tight knit group of friends and family noticed it as well. He looked suave in his white shirt with black tie and black vest. The diamond cufflinks on his shirt cuffs sparkled in the light of the room as he held his drink.

Jolene entered the room and sat at their table, dressed in a low cut striking scarlet gown, accenting her perfectly styled raven dark hair and eyes. Around her neck was a glistening gold choker. She looked stunning and she seemed to know the effect she was having on the men in the room, who appeared to be dazzled by her.

"You look beautiful this evening, Jolene," remarked Fred.

"Thank you, I am looking forward to being able to purchase the latest fashions from Paris once again."

"Indeed," he agreed. Turning toward Kate, he said, "And you, Kate, look beguiling in your gown. Did Ken pick it out for you?"

Kate looked up and smiled. "Thank you, yes, he likes blue and has an eye for fashion, as you can tell by his outfit. He bought the tie to match my gown."

Jolene descended into silence, a sulky expression marring her pretty features. "I didn't realize that blue was a color he was partial to. It is so ordinary," she said.

The implication was that not only the color of the dress, but Kate herself was very ordinary and Jolene was pointing it out. This woman was frustrating, but she wasn't going to let it spoil the evening.

Dinner was delicious: light bisque, fresh salad, followed by filet of sole, green peas and for dessert, strawberry tarts with whipped cream. Conversation was light and pleasant. Afterward, the orchestra set up for dancing. Ken stood and held out his hand. "Dance with me, Kate."

"I would love to."

He led her to the dance floor. It was a slow dance and the closeness of Ken's body warmed her heart. He danced beautifully, another thing he was good at. She realized he probably excelled at everything he attempted. The intimacy of the interaction made her fantasize that she really was Ken's intended and they were there on holiday, not to investigate a murder but to simply enjoy the time spent together and attend a lavish wedding of a close family member.

The dance came to an end, bringing Kate out of her pleasant daydream. They sauntered back to their seats at the table. Kate noticed Andrew was sitting by himself at a nearby table, looking forlorn. She immediately walked over to him and sat down.

"Andrew, it's nice to see you again," she said, unsure of what sort of topic to bring up that would interest him."

"Ah, the lovely Kate. Sorry I'm feeling so down right now. So many memories. It could have been my wedding and my after-party."

"Why don't we have a go at a dance?" Kate asked him, hoping to cheer him up.

"Why not give it a try" he responded, and gallantly bowed at her and took her hand. They enjoyed a lively jitter-bug, and afterward she invited him to sit at their table, which he did.

As the next song began, Dexter approached Kate and held out his hand. "May I have the pleasure of this dance?"

"Certainly," Kate replied as she took his hand, got up from her chair and joined Dexter on the dance floor.

Jolene decided to take advantage of the situation, seeing her chance to dance with Ken. With not so much words, but body language, glancing at the dance floor and then back to Ken, she indicated she would like a dance. Ken obliged and the both of them were soon dancing to another slow and perfectly orchestrated rendition of a popular 1940's love song.

Dexter danced well, Kate could not deny it, but soon he was back into his investigative mode, which Kate had learned to evasively deflect. Instead of the usual polite niceties one would bring up during a dance, Dexter started his prodding again asking, "What is your full name, Kate?"

She laughed it off, "Surely you aren't writing a piece about me! Your readers would find it very boring."

"No, I'm not, I'm just curious. I have friends in Newbury. None of them have acknowledged knowing someone by the name of Kate."

"My name is Katherine Richter."

"Isn't Richter a German name?"

"It is."

"But you were here throughout the war. Wasn't that a problem?"

"No. No one had or has now ever questioned where my loyalties lie."

"There was so much talk of Nazi spies being turned to become spies for the Allies."

"So I have heard."

"But everyone knows that you could never really turn a Nazi spy."

Kate almost gasped at this ridiculous ignorant statement. "If that was true, there would have been no D-day invasion. That depended on double agents convincing the Nazi regime that an allied invasion of France was planned for Calais so the Nazis could be prepared, instead of Normandy, where they were not. I've read that all Nazi spies that were found out, were turned or captured."

Dexter looked at her.

"Anyway, that's what I've read," Kate said looking at Dexter with confident eyes.

The dance ended, to Kate's relief. Just as she was headed back to the table, Dexter grabbed her hand. "Care to step outside for a breath of fresh air?"

Kate didn't want to but was more afraid that he would continue their discussion at the table, so she agreed and followed him outside to the terrace.

Leaning against the wall of the hotel, Dexter put a hand to his breast pocket and drew out a cigarette case. "Cigarette?"

"No, thank you."

He opened the case, took out a cigarette and put it between his lips as he searched for his lighter. "Yes," he said, lighting his cigarette, "I did know about the spies."

Not as handsome as Ken in the traditional sense, he did possess a certain magnetism, confidence and roguish charm. Kate could not deny her attraction to him. Dark hair and penetrating eyes probably got him a long way in his profession. People would be likely to confide in him, especially women. He looked at Kate with an inquiring look.

"How long did you say you have known Ken?"

"As I have told you, we have been dating for several months."

"But here you are, outside with me."

"I....."

He then leaned over and whispered in her ear, "I think you were a spy."

Kate instinctively jumped back. "That is absurd! You are delusional." she exclaimed as she turned to head back to the door which led into the ballroom.

Dexter grabbed her arm gently, bringing her back to face him.

"Relax. I think you were working for our side. Otherwise Robertson would have arrested you by now."

"Who?"

"Robertson. The government agent that has been following you around all the time you've been in London. The gentleman with the red bow tie. He asked questions about you at the library when he saw you through the window as you stopped by to wave goodbye to me, which made me suspicious. He seemed to recognize you."

"I see."

"MP Edward Aylesworth was asking questions about you also. Well, after all, he is a Member of Parliament and has to know who he is associating with."

"Of course he does."

"Who are you really?"

"I don't believe I need to answer that, Mr. Flynn. I am who I say I am. Mr. Robertson must be mistaking me for someone else, and Mr. Aylesworth will not be disappointed if he is associating with me."

"Call me Dexter, we're all friends here, aren't we?"

"Friends don't interrogate each other endlessly trying to make them out to be something they are not."

"Fair enough. Please accept my apologies," he said with a charming smile.

Dexter then moved in very close to her, gently moving her against the wall, putting his arm above her to pull her in, his lit cigarette between his fingers. She could smell his aftershave and was intoxicated by the fragrance and his closeness.

"It's just the journalist in me. I can't turn it off."

"I really must get back to Ken." This man was relentless, and it was hard to resist his charms, but something about him, or maybe it was her attraction to him, made her want to escape as quickly as possible.

From where they were standing, Dexter moved his arm so that Kate could see Ken dancing close and intimately with Jolene. It looked like Ken whispered something in her ear which made her laugh.

"I think he's rather occupied," Dexter commented.

"So he is."

Then he leaned close to Kate's face and kissed her on the lips. The prudent thing to do would be to break away but, for a brief moment, she responded, then pushed him gently away. That kiss, a post-war indulgence, stealing a kiss at a party, felt like life as it should be after years of a terrible, brutal war. It was quite pleasant and disturbing at the same time. And, after all, she rationalized, she was only pretending to be Ken's girlfriend which, somehow, she thought that Dexter must have figured out.

Dexter looked at Kate with inquisitive eyes, as if surprised at his own boldness and her reaction to it.

"I better not get caught trying to seduce another man's girl, let's go back in," he said softly as he released his grip on her.

She composed herself. "Good night, Dexter," she said, looking straight in his face. "Oh my goodness, you'll need this," she added as she pulled out the handkerchief that was in his vest pocket, "please wipe the lipstick off your face before you go back in." He laughed and did so. She then turned and walked back into the hotel. Dexter stood still against the wall, watching her and wondering.

Unbeknown to them, more than one pair of peering eyes had witnessed the entire encounter.

CHAPTER 20

The rest of the dance was uneventful. Kate danced a few more times with Ken, one with Edward Aylesworth who at least acted nicer toward her than when he was introduced, and other gentlemen whose names she forgot as soon as the dances were over.

Jolene was occupied as well, as she was not at a loss for male attention. Kate surmised that Ken decided that if he paid too much attention to Jolene, people would question his engagement to her. Perhaps if she wasn't there, Jolene and Ken would become an item. She suddenly felt out of place, like she was intruding on this circle of family and friends. That caused a strong pang of jealousy to run through her, although she knew she had no right to be jealous, since she couldn't claim a real relationship with Ken. The only relationship she had with the man was pretend, and perhaps, in her own mind.

The man with the red bow tie, who Kate now knew was a Mr. Robertson, had left. Why on earth was the man asking about her? What ties might she have to a government agent? She decided the next time she saw him, if she could get him alone, she might ask him directly. Dexter was also at the party, but remained sitting at the bar, drinking beer and discussing world events with the bartender. Thank goodness he was leaving her alone!

As she and Ken danced, Kate noticed Edward Aylesworth moved to the bar and slapped Dexter on the shoulder as he offered to buy him a drink. The bartender served whiskeys to them both and they talked intently, looking over now and then at Ken and Kate.

"Does Dexter know MP Aylesworth well?" Kate asked Ken as they were swirling around and she found a chance to gain his ear.

"Yes, I believe they go way back. It looks like they are talking politics."

From the way they both were looking at her as they talked, Kate didn't think they were talking politics at all.

As it got late, and the crowd started to thin, the remaining party-goers left the hotel and moved to Fred's house, where Fred had arranged an after-party get-together. Kate was relieved to find Dexter had not followed the group. Sir Fred pulled out the phonograph and put on some background music and the caterers he hired were prepared with drinks and hors d'oeuvres on trays. The mood was festive and the conversation was light. Looking at the guests and hearing the pleasant conversation and innocent laughter, the idea that any of these people could be guilty of a crime so horrible as Natalie's murder seemed to border on lunacy.

As the evening wore down and the guests started to leave, Kate said her goodnights to Fred and the few remaining guests. Not being able to find Ken to tell him goodnight, she went up to her room. The head of the staircase opened on the central point of the main upper corridor, which was like a large tee, its two branches both lined with windows facing over the back lawn of the house. Kate's room was in the far corner, at the end of the right arm of the tee.

After returning to her room, she proceeded to get undressed and ready for bed. The bathroom next to her room was occupied, so, wrapping herself in her black silk robe and bringing along her toiletry kit, she set out in search of the other bathroom on the floor. She knew it was on the far end of the corridor by Ken's room. After washing the make-up off her face and brushing her teeth, she quietly let herself out of the bathroom and walked cautiously along the now-darkened corridor. The house had seemed to settle into silence for the night.

She went softly by Ken's room and was almost past before she realized that someone was standing, still and quiet, just inside the doorway of Ken's room. Startled, she glanced inside.

It was two people. They had not noticed Kate, and for a good reason. They were in one another's arms, kissing passionately.

The woman was Jolene. From the dim light of the window, Kate recognized her dark hair and her scarlet dress even before her perfume reached her senses. She recognized the man as well. It was Ken.

Hurriedly she looked away and continued softly down the corridor towards her room. She closed the door and stood inside, her back against the door, realizing one of her headaches was coming on. A mixture of embarrassment and anger swept over her, even though she felt it was irrational. Ken had never led her to believe he had a romantic interest in her and they were only pretending to be a couple.

This was so frustrating. She had volunteered for this mission, but she could not help but wonder whether her life would ever settle down and not involve secrecy and deception. Was love out of her grasp? She had feelings for Ken, and apparently had mistakenly thought he had feelings for her. Or if he did, it looks like he had succumbed to Jolene's charms. Maybe it would be best for him to marry in his own social circle, as Dexter had not too politely pointed out.

She sat down on the bed and took a deep breath. It wasn't the end of the world, she was a survivor and would make it past this, she rationalized as her eyes filled with tears. Then her thoughts turned to Dexter. Men! He probably was only interested in a story and the mystery surrounding her. No doubt he had used his charms to gather information throughout his career. Dexter, Ken, Jolene – she couldn't wait to get away from the lot of them! She would pack up and leave within a fortnight, murder solved or not.

From inside her purse she found two aspirin, took them, got into bed and tried to sleep, knowing it would be a restless night.

CHAPTER 21

Ken left the house early the next morning, before anyone else had arisen. He hadn't told Kate everything about what he had been doing during his stints to London while she was recuperating at the cottage. The truth was his business interests had been taking a lot of his attention.

The Michaels family had old money, that was true, but the large estate it had owned for centuries in Lancashire had become quite expensive to maintain. It was decided some years before the war that the most prudent thing to do was sell off the family holdings, including the beautiful estate. This decision was made during the time Ken was attending Oxford.

The old patriarch of the family, Robert Michaels, had been ill for a number of years and passed on several years earlier. His sons, Albert and Fred, quickly realized the extensive time and effort it took to take care of their large family estate and were easily able to sell the estate and split the money equally. Fred had bought his house, and Albert had purchased a well-built stately 3,000 square foot home several miles away, in which to house himself and his family. In addition, he purchased a cottage in Bath which he and his family could use as a summer retreat. He also set up a trust fund for his children, thus providing a sizeable and steady income for both Ken and his brother Allen.

The cottage in Newbury was an investment Ken had made for himself after graduating college, with the thought of leasing it out or selling it for a profit eventually. However, instead of letting it out or putting it on the market, he had decided to stay there himself occasionally for a break from the city.

And then Natalie had been murdered. Nothing could ever be the same again. Ken had been very close to his sister and her death devastated him. It distressed him greatly that the police had no idea who had committed the crime. At that time Ken had looked at all his associates and relatives with suspicion. When war broke out, he made a rather hasty decision to join the RAF. The cottage would remain empty while he was gone.

It was convenient that he had held on to the cottage as it also served as a refuge for keeping Kate away from prying eyes. By the time Kate arrived, he had it furnished and looking well lived-in.

Another investment which he, his brother, dad and uncle had made was in the plastics business. Plastics were a growing commodity and new usages for the material were growing exponentially. Since Ken had the business degree, he was tasked with making sure the London manufacturing company in which they had an interest was thriving.

As well, there had been some investments in India. Franklin had been the instigator for the plan and had convinced the family to invest in a tea plantation in India. Now that he was in London, Ken dropped in to see the family accountant for a status report, while Kate was otherwise occupied.

"I'm not so sure things are going well with the plantation," Franklin had responded to Ken's question on the state of his investments.

"What exactly do you mean?" Ken was a bit exasperated with the man, who never said things directly, instead talking around every issue.

"Well, it looks like there is some fallout from the war."

"What sort of fallout?"

"Your initial investment has fallen somewhere around 50%. Sorry, it's not like I can control anything going on there. Workers are rebelling. They are demanding independence and soon India will no longer be under British rule. They could privatize any companies operating there at any time."

Ken knew that George Cresswell, Andrew's father, had also invested in the properties along with them.

"And the Cresswell investment?"

"You know I can't talk about other people's money. But I can tell you he's not happy right now."

Ken felt a sinking feeling in the pit of his stomach. He'd been the one talking up the investment to George. Too bad George hadn't also decided to get into plastics or petroleum products. Ken had seen the potential for the new products and those businesses were lucrative.

"What about transferring the India interests into some businesses producing colorful fabrics or spices?" Ken asked Franklin.

"I can check into it. I think you'd be wise to pull out now and count your losses."

"I'm not quite ready for that. We'll talk again. Please research those options for me."

As Ken left their meeting, it occurred to him he might be able to help Andrew get out of his doldrums. Perhaps he might be interested in a management position at the plastics manufacturing company. Ken felt sure it would be more interesting for Andrew than working at the bank. He knew that Andrew was very intelligent and had a business degree. He made a note to talk to Andrew about it the next time they met.

Lost Secrets

CHAPTER 22

Franklin breathed a sigh of relief after Ken left his office. It was hard to keep secrets, but in his position, it was essential. He was tasked with investing wealthy people's money and he took his job very seriously. It was always a gamble. Sometimes you lost, sometimes you won. In his view, though, it was fair game to pick who would win. Some paid him more than others, those were the ones to impress.

He wasn't sure about Ken. His family had money, but he was cautious with his investments. And he never suspected Franklin, the whole family trusted him.

Leading a double life was harder than one would think. Pinching a little bit here and there allowed him to purchase a large house, buy an estate in the country, take expensive vacations. But these luxuries had to be hidden away. Ostensibly he lived in a small London flat, a bachelor with a dull life. No-one knew about his flings with ladies of a certain profession. Women would be his downfall, he was certain.

He had covered up tracks for a number of clients through the years. He was worried about being exposed with the investigations about the Natalie Michaels affair. He had to act as if he didn't know anything about it, when the police came calling. No, just the family accountant, nothing more. No, Natalie had no investments with him. No, he had no idea of anyone being upset with her.

But there were some who had serious involvement with unsavory schemes overseas during the war. He didn't become involved, but he knew it was a lucrative business. He wanted to disclose this information but worried that if he did, he could open up floodgates to being investigated himself and then his business dealings and crimes would be exposed.

He had an idea of who had "removed" her and why. But he would never voice those suspicions, just keep everything he knew to his plain old quirky self. Being a loner was the best way to be. A loner with well-kept secrets.

CHAPTER 23

Kate was relieved that Ken had already left the house when she got up that morning. She was to attend a woman's luncheon at the Ness Hotel. Gwendolyn insisted that she go, however, after seeing Ken and Jolene kissing last evening, Kate was not too keen on eating lunch at the same table as Jolene. She put on makeup to cover the dark circles under her eyes from a sleepless night and slipped into a dress appropriate for the luncheon.

The frequent gatherings held at the Hotel caused Kate to wonder if Fred didn't have a vested interest in the establishment, perhaps as part-owner. Travis kindly drove her to the entrance and as she walked in, she looked for Gwendolyn, but didn't see her at first glance.

"Good afternoon, Kate."

Kate turned to see Amanda approaching and was very happy to see her. She always made her feel welcome and accepted.

"Good afternoon, Amanda," she said warmly taking her hand.

"Gwendolyn said we would be expecting you, it is so nice to see you again."

"Very nice to see you as well."

"Our table is just over here." Amanda turned and made her way through the crowded room toward a table in the corner, glancing back to make sure Kate was following. At the table sat Gwendolyn and Andrew's mother, Elaine. Kate was introduced to Elaine, whom she had not met formally before. Elaine seemed like a calm person without an agenda, and she smiled politely at Kate.

The only space available for her to sit was between Amanda and Gwendolyn, which felt like a comfortable place to be. Just when she started to relax, she saw Jolene coming toward the table with Evelyn's mother, Lenora. Lenora had a strong resemblance to her daughter, Evelyn. Evelyn had been a lovely bride, and Kate hoped she and Thomas would be happy together. Interesting though, did Jolene and Lenora arrive together? What was Jolene's relationship with Evelyn and her family? There was so much to learn. She had a new resolve and wasn't going to let Ken's actions stop her from helping his family find Natalie's killer.

"Lovely day," Kate said as Jolene and Lenora took their seats at the table and exchanged pleasant hellos.

It was, of course, the picture of politeness. They all made pleasant, superficial conversation, but as the drinks and appetizers arrived, Kate began to feel out of place. Jolene and the others talked about people that Kate didn't know.

Lenora mentioned that she thought Mrs. Patel had been invited and at that, again, Kate noticed that Amanda's face froze.

"Mrs. Patel has been invited?" Amanda inquired. "Why?"

"The Patels are moving back to London and I want to welcome them," Lenora said, not mentioning that she and her husband had business ties with them. "She should be here soon."

"I think I'll visit the powder room," Amanda said to the guests at the table. "If you'll excuse me."

"I'll come with you," Kate said. "My make-up could use a bit of freshening up."

Kate followed Amanda into the washroom. Purple velvet chairs were lined up in front of a long mirror. There was a woman looking in the mirror, applying lipstick, so Kate took out the powder compact from her handbag and carefully began applying powder to her face."

The woman left, and Amanda turned to Kate. She had tears in her eyes. "It was my fear that they would move back to London," she said.

"I'm sorry. Is there anything I can do to help?"

Amanda composed herself and sat in one of the velvet chairs. Kate sat next to her and turned to offer support.

"I suppose you have heard that I had a romantic relationship with Raj."

Kate didn't want to seem like a gossip, but she confessed, "Ken did mention it at the reception."

Then the bombshell.

"There was a child. I gave birth to a son."

Kate almost gasped, her eyes widened, but she calmly replied, "Where is the child now?"

"He died."

"Oh my God, I'm so sorry! What happened?"

"Raj and I couldn't marry because his family had an arranged marriage set up for him. He didn't want to disappoint them and was unwilling to turn his back on his family and their tradition. My parents had just come back from India so they passed off my son as a child they adopted there. As you can imagine, they wanted to avoid a scandal. It wasn't a scandal to me, but I had no say in the matter. My father has important business interests and insisted it could not be known that his unmarried daughter had a child."

"Oh dear."

"His name was Daniel. He had a nanny and they never told him that I was his mum. I loved him so much, he was the light of my life. He believed I was his sister. During the war, feeling he was unsafe because of the constant airstrikes by the Germans, the rationing, all the uncertainty of living in London, and afraid the allies might lose the war, my family and I allowed the Patel's to take my son to India. He was only five and he died there from typhoid fever. They didn't bring his little body back here for Christian burial which again broke my heart."

Kate's hand went to her throat. "That must have been devastating for you."

"I hadn't seen the Patel's or Raj since then, but then they were at the wedding. It's so dreadful to be reminded."

"When did this happen?"

"At the start of the war, during the blitz."

Kate was astonished to hear about so much tragedy that had happened to this family before and during the war. Losing Natalie, then losing Daniel, with Ken and Andrew in the forces, not knowing if they would ever return. She had a renewed respect and admiration for the resilience of this family and their countrymen. She didn't know what to say to make Amanda feel better.

Amanda continued, "I'm sorry to have burdened you with my problems but it really helps to talk, and you seem like a caring person who doesn't judge or hold onto prejudices."

"Talking with you could never be a burden," Kate responded, gently touching Amanda's hand. "I'm so glad you confided in me. I hope we can be friends."

Amanda dabbed the tears from her eyes, "I know we will be friends." She cheered up a bit as she considered Kate's position. "Not only are we going to be friends," Amanda said warmly, "we are going to be family – once you are married to my cousin Ken."

"You're right, we will be family," Kate agreed, with a sinking feeling in her gut that it was too bad she wasn't going to marry into the family. It would have been nice to be related to Amanda.

Seeing the changed look on Kate's face, Amanda said, "We haven't scared you away, have we?"

"No, of course not, we'll be family and friends."

Kate was not in the mood to divulge any of her own private concerns. Amanda would be more than shocked if she knew her background and her ruse to help Ken. She also wasn't going to share with Amanda that their discussion was a welcome diversion from Jolene and what she had witnessed the night before.

"We should get back to the table," Amanda said as she stood up to leave. The two walked back to the group with confident strides until they realized that Mrs. Patel had arrived.

Amanda immediately said she had a terrible headache and could not stay for lunch. As she left, Kate sat back down at the table. No-one seemed to be aware of the reason behind Amanda's departure, Kate noted, or if they did, they didn't mention it, other than concern for her. That was somewhat comforting.

The luncheon was excellent – light and cool – salads and sandwiches with fruit and meringue supplemented by delicious tea and cakes.

At one point, someone inadvertently mentioned Natalie. Kate could see something in Mrs. Patel's eyes. Was it fear or guilt? *That woman knows something*, Kate thought. Was it only because of her grandson's death, or did she know something about the murder of Natalie Michaels?

CHAPTER 24

The luncheon ended and Gwendolyn gave Kate a lift back to Fred's house. She was a rather wild driver, careening quickly through intersections, hardly watching for other vehicles, and she seemed oblivious to Kate's hand clutching firmly on the handle attached at the side of the car above the door. She chatted cheerfully with Kate about her new dog, a Pomeranian she had named Puff. When they arrived in front of Fred's house, she stopped the car and paused, looking directly at Kate and taking her hand.

"Dear Kate, we are warming up to you every day. Now that we're alone I can talk freely to you. As you can imagine, I terribly miss my daughter, Natalie. We were so disappointed the local constabulary was unable to find her killer. They were preoccupied with the war looming in the horizon. It's a horrible thing to lose a child." She was close to tears but her strict upbringing encouraged her to cover her emotions.

Kate listened attentively, nodding her head.

"I understand your background involves some sort of spy work. You also went to college, so you have some smarts about you. Both Albert and I hope you are able to uncover secrets and find clues that may help bring her killer to justice. I don't have confidence in the police, or, I'm sorry to say, Detective Spencer. He seems to be only making a half-hearted effort."

"I promise I will do my best to help, using all of my skills. I sincerely enjoy your family and spending time with Ken, although as you know, we aren't really engaged."

"Well, not yet anyway," she said with a sly smile.

Kate smiled in return and, changing the subject, said, "Would you care to come in?"

"No, thank you dear, I have a bridge game this afternoon."

"Alright, thank you so much for the lovely luncheon."

"You are more than welcome. Give my regards to Ken and Fred."

"I will."

As Kate entered the house, she put down her purse and went up to her room briefly to change into more casual clothes. Wondering if Fred was about, she began wandering through the house. She found him in his library, reading a book, relaxing in a comfortable chair by the window. This looked like her chance to confront him.

"Good afternoon, Fred. Gwendolyn sends her regards."

"How nice," Fred remarked in an uninterested tone of voice, without looking up.

"Where is Ken?"

"He was out on business early this morning, then came back and changed clothes to go play tennis again with Andrew. It's a lovely day for it."

"It certainly is."

Kate brought up a chair and sat down near him. The room was cozy and warm, with the same lavish look of every other room in the house. It had Victorian period leather chairs, and expensive sets of bound volumes on oak bookshelves. There was a thick pile carpet and a richly carved desk in the corner. The entire south and east walls were lined with books from top to bottom, and Kate thought that maybe one day she'd like to pull out a few and catch up on some reading.

Fred turned and looked at her through the top of his reading glasses, getting the feeling this was not going to be a casual conversation.

"Yes, Kate, how can I help you?"

"Fred, I've been meaning to talk to you. It's about something I found out at the city library when I was there the other day."

"Is that so?" He closed the book, took off his glasses and set them both on a small side table next to him.

"Yes, I came across an article written about Natalie's murder. The article specifically said that you were interviewed at the scene by a constable immediately after you came home and found her body. The constable asked if anything had been missing and you said that only her papers, her journal, and her diamond engagement ring was not on her hand. The part about the missing ring was not in the official statement that you gave the police later."

Fred said nothing and just looked at Kate. He reached for his cigarette case, took one out and lit it up. He took a long, slow puff, looking away from her.

"I don't mean to be impertinent, but I'd like to know what happened. Please don't think I'm nosy. The only reason I'm asking and trying to help Ken is that it means so much to him, to find out who killed his sister. You must understand that he needs to have closure. Bringing the killer to justice will help him get it. Then he can sleep at night and fulfill a promise that he made to himself."

Fred's face started to turn red and tighten as he said, "I can see where this is going. Have you mentioned this to Ken?"

"No."

At that, Fred's face relaxed and he looked like he was going to be more forthcoming.

"Care to explain?" Kate asked, determined to find out the truth.

"No, not really."

He took another drag on his cigarette and the smoke filtered up to the ceiling.

"I honestly have the sincerest of intentions, Fred. It appears that you might be protecting someone. Are you?"

"Perhaps."

He was a bit stubborn, and she'd have to try harder. This man was a mystery, changing from sociable and friendly to decided aloofness. She would have to be more direct with her suspicions.

"My thoughts are that Jolene stole the ring."

"I do think Jolene stole the ring," he finally confessed, shaking his head. "It was obvious. She was in love with Andrew and insanely jealous when Natalie and Andrew became engaged, with the emphasis on insanely. I don't know how she managed it, but I'm sure she took it."

That was a rather major admission. She was glad he opened up to her. "I see," she responded. "But, if she was in love with Andrew then, I don't understand why they don't rekindle their relationship now."

"I think she has tried but he isn't in an emotional position to have a relationship presently and he knows it. Maybe with time he will be. God willing."

"Do you think he suspects her of killing Natalie?"

"I think not," he answered.

"It sounds like you don't think Jolene murdered Natalie either. How can you be sure?" Kate felt cold and calculating asking him so many questions, but that was what she was there for.

"She did not murder Natalie. She should have returned the ring right away, explained how she came to be in possession of it, and come clean. I'm sure she eventually will. It was an irrational thing to do. I didn't want to implicate her. I didn't mention it again, otherwise it would distract the detectives from finding the actual perpetrator by wasting time investigating her. She didn't have an alibi, being home alone that evening. She is fragile and an interrogation would be too much for her. She wouldn't be able to bear it."

"That makes sense. Please go on," Kate said, glad she was finally gaining new information.

"You'd probably find out with more research anyway," he conceded. Gazing past her, he continued, "Jolene's mother died when she was young. She basically had to raise herself, poor thing, she's had a tough go of it, and I believe she is desperate to find love and acceptance. She may come off as a tiger but deep inside she's hurting."

"You seem to know a lot about her. What exactly is your relationship to Jolene?"

"I had a special friendship with her mother, who was a very kind and sweet woman. I'll never forget her." Kate could see sadness in his eyes.

"Tell me if I'm overstepping boundaries - are you Jolene's father?" Kate did think she was out-of-line by this question, but Fred didn't seem to take offense.

"No, I'm not her father but I feel an obligation to look after her, if for no other reason than for my respect and love for her mother. My relationship with Lydia didn't begin until after Jolene was born. Jolene's father was and still is away most of the time. Jolene was brought up by nannies. She had money but no love or affection from her father. He is not a warm and caring man. She was an only child. I try to fill in the gap by being a sort of uncle to her. I take her out to events, buy her presents for her birthday, things such as that to make her feel like she has a family that loves her."

"That is very kind of you. Does she appreciate your attention and kindness?"

"Yes, she does. She reciprocates when she can. She looks after me when I'm ill. Last month, I had a terrible toothache. Anna had just brought in some cherries but I couldn't eat them because of my bad tooth. Jolene went to the kitchen and pitted them so I could more easily enjoy them. Then she took me to the dentist later."

Kate was surprised that the woman that was shooting daggers at her with her eyes would make such a kind gesture. "I can see why you want to protect her."

Fred looked out the window. Kate realized that quite likely Fred had been in love with Jolene's mother. Perhaps that was why he never married.

"What happened to Lydia? Did she become ill?"

"No, she fell down a flight of steep stairs at the house they lived in. It was a bad fall and she sustained internal injuries. She never had a chance."

"Did anyone take her to the hospital?"

"No one was home at the time. She wasn't found until hours later and by that time, she was gone."

"Accident?"

"That was the official report. I have my doubts."

"Her husband?"

"Well, I've always wondered if he found out about our affair. I assumed he did and pushed her to her death. He is a violent and vindictive man. I think he was at home and he did not have an alibi for the afternoon when the fall had happened."

"Didn't the authorities question the accident or have suspicions of him?"

"Apparently not, they just ruled the death as an accident."

These upper-crust society folks are pretty ruthless. How hypocritical they are to look down their noses at other people, Kate thought. "Fred, I am so sorry. That is awful."

"Well, it's all the past. We can only move forward and try to lead better lives."

If this was true, Kate wondered if Fred carried a lot of guilt. Maybe that had a lot to do with why he filled the role of Jolene's benevolent uncle and substitute parent.

There were a few moments of silent reflection, then Fred spoke, "If and when Ken finds out about the ring, please help me convince him that the ring had nothing to do with the murder and that it does not make Jolene a bad person. I strongly believe that Jolene did a silly and compulsive thing, out of feelings of jealousy and loss, that's all. Promise me."

"I promise." *Did I just promise to defend my romantic rival? Should I be more charitable toward Jolene? Do I unconsciously hope she's the perpetrator? My life is becoming more like a Shakespearean tragedy every day, or is it a comedy?*

Fred rose, put his cigarette out and looked like he was about to leave the room, but Kate wasn't finished with the conversation. In fact, she had another theory to discuss with hm.

"Fred, I'm still wondering about the ring. Did you see Jolene take it or did she confess to you that she did?

"No, I've just assumed. Jewelry and sparkling things are her downfall and that combined with her jealousy, it added up."

"I'm trying to consider all the options. Could it be possible that Natalie and Andrew had a bad row on that fateful night and she gave Andrew back the ring and ended the relationship?"

"I've never thought of that." He paused for a moment, sat back down in his chair and said slowly, "You know, I've never thought of that as a potential reason for the ring's disappearance. Anything is possible, I suppose. They did have occasional disagreements, as all couples do, and Andrew did volunteer for the infantry soon after the murder."

"You never know what people who have been rejected will do in the heat of passion. Do you think Andrew might have been so hurt and angry that he killed Natalie?" It sounded absurd to Kate, but one never knew.

"It's possible, but doubtful if you ask me. His grief seemed very genuine at the funeral."

"Even if he did murder her, not as a planned attack, but in a fit of uncontrollable anger, he would feel genuine remorse and grief. Did he ever ask about the ring, ask for it back?"

"No, come to think of it, he didn't. And he would be strong enough to strangle her. Jolene wouldn't be."

CHAPTER 25

Fred considered this new theory. Then steps were heard outside the library and Ken came in full of energy, having finished his tennis game.

"What's this? Having an obviously serious conversation without including me?"

"Please take a seat, Ken," Fred suggested as he pointed to an empty chair and said, "How was your tennis match?"

"Very nice, a perfect day for it, I tried to let Andrew win at least one game, but my competitive streak wouldn't have it. He is getting better and, I'll tell you, it was a narrow victory this time."

"I'm so glad you had a good day, and I'm glad to hear Andrew is improving," Kate said, smiling at Ken. There was an awkward silent moment while Ken seemed to be waiting to hear what the two were talking about when he walked in.

Kate decided to break the ice about what was foremost on their minds. "Ken, we were discussing the murder," she explained and then continued, "And surprisingly your uncle is letting up on his dislike of our investigation."

"So, you're finally going to support our search?" he inquired of Fred.

"I've relented," he admitted. "I see now how much it means to you to have that kind of closure. I've got nothing to hide and will cooperate fully with you. Fire away."

Kate took the lead, "Fred, who knew that you would be gone for a few days when the murder took place?" That would be a good place to start, she decided.

"I'd say quite a lot of people knew. Everyone I know was aware of the conference and that I was planning to attend."

"I see. Were Mr. Patel, Franklin, Edward or George with you at the conference?"

"No, Mr. Patel wasn't involved with the organization that was having the conference. Franklin was out of town on business and George was ill."

"Did Elaine confirm that George was ill?

"Yes, she said he was very ill with the flu. Also, I believe his doctor was interviewed."

"How about Franklin?"

"I assume the investigators checked out his alibi to confirm where he was."

"You said that Franklin is your accountant, is that right?"

"Yes."

"Do you ever have an independent person audit your books?"

"No, surely you're not suggesting…no, I don't think that would be necessary."

"I'm just looking at all avenues. I'm certainly not accusing anyone, but we need to keep in mind there are numerous possibilities as to who might have had the means and the motive." Hopefully she wasn't prying too much. Fred seemed familiar with the investigation and this was the first time he was willing to discuss it. Ken was just letting her run with it, listening intently.

"I have absolute trust in Franklin, as do most of my friends and Ken here."

Kate felt free to ask more questions since Fred was now willing to offer all information he knew.

"How about Edward?"

"He was home and his wife, Julia. She vouched for him."

"Are you sure that both Travis and Anna had left for the day? Did they have alibis?"

"Yes, their alibis did check out. Besides, they both loved Natalie."

"Dexter knew Natalie as well. Could Natalie have fancied either Dexter or Travis, perhaps one of them was a rival for her relationship to Andrew?"

"Possibly Dexter, but not Travis. Travis had a love interest at the time. A darling girl to whom he is now married. Besides, he was young, only sixteen then."

"Ken, another avenue of thought that Fred and I were discussing before you came in was the possibility that Natalie could have broken off her engagement with Andrew."

This got Ken's back up. "Kate, what are you suggesting?" he asked, concern in his voice.

Fred chipped in, "It's true that Dexter and Natalie spent a lot of time together, but I don't think there was anything romantic going on between them."

Another moment of silence ensued, with tensions high in all three. Fred and Kate knew that any suggestion that Andrew was involved would deeply upset Ken.

With his elbows on the arms of the chairs and looking at Kate, Fred finally said, "We might as well tell Ken about the ring and what we were discussing when he came in the room. Only the missing ring will explain why we considered that possibly Natalie and Andrew broke up and why our thoughts were directed toward Andrew as a possible suspect."

"What ring?" Ken was surprised by this. "Do you mean Natalie's engagement ring?"

"The very one," Fred answered.

"What about it? I don't recall even thinking about it. After she died it was such a horrid time and I was in shock. When I took her passport and locket, I don't remember seeing a ring. Is it missing?"

"It is missing," Kate said. "But perhaps it had been at the jewelers being sized and never picked up. I discovered it was missing after reading some articles at the library the other day."

"The library? Why haven't you mentioned it to me before?"

"I'm sorry, I just thought about it today and the possible implications of it."

"Well, I'm glad you finally shared it with me. We'll find out who the jeweler was, let's start our investigation tomorrow."

Kate agreed and true to her word, said nothing about the likelihood that Jolene had taken it, as she had promised Fred she would do. She stood up and told Ken and Fred she needed some quiet time to think and went to her room. The truth was that she felt a headache coming on. She took two aspirin.

Laying on her bed she closed her eyes. Memories came flooding back.

The telegraph machine went clickity-clack as another sheet of paper with lies came in. Herr Kliegen always invented things that he knew leadership wanted to hear. She snatched it up and took it to her desk. Carefully she transferred the information to the form her supervisor had asked for.

The next telegram was in English, an intercepted communication. This one didn't make any sense, so she embellished it and changed it in her translation to German so that it sounded important and somewhat feasible. Day after day working on these translations were driving her crazy. Knowing that innocent people were being executed, young men sent out to certain death with no say in the matter. It wasn't right.

Her heart had led her to this place in Germany, but she wished she could do more to help the Allies. And one of her contacts, Mikael, was missing. She hoped he hadn't been discovered, as that would lead to his torture and murder. She knew he would never put her at risk. All of them were under such stress. It was wearing her down, she wondered how she could bear it another day.

The pounding in her head stopped and she fell asleep for an hour. She awoke with a start and realized it was time for their evening meal. She washed her face and headed downstairs.

CHAPTER 26

After dinner, Kate sat on the veranda on the lawn behind Sir Fred's house, the very place where Natalie had been murdered six years ago. It was a warm summer evening with only the faintest of breezes rustling through the rambling roses that hung over the awning. She wanted a little time to herself to think about everything. She wanted so much to help the Michaels family bring the killer to justice. Being an outsider, it was easy for her to remove herself from any family or friendship ties and look at potential suspects from an objective point of view, something that was obviously more difficult for Ken and Fred. She could tell by the way they reacted from the discussions they had earlier. She had discovered her thinking was analytical, probably one of the reasons she had been a successful agent.

Organizing the potential suspects in her mind, she first thought of Jolene, who had been in love with Andrew. Andrew didn't return her feelings and instead was engaged to Natalie. Jolene had a motive, jealousy is a strong emotion. If Natalie had inadvertently said something that upset Jolene and anger overcome her, perhaps she snapped. But somehow Kate didn't feel like that was plausible. Also, did she have the strength to strangle someone who could fight back?

She moved to Andrew, Natalie's fiancé. No-one had mentioned any discord between him and Natalie other than an occasional argument that Fred knew about, and there had been no mention of infidelity. He still seemed upset about her death, and that didn't strike Kate as being a sign of a killer. Did they have an argument in which Natalie threw her ring at him and said the engagement was off? That could provoke a rage in a young man in love, and at a stressful time of impending war. Could it have been a crime of passion? Anna didn't seem to find Andrew a suitable match for Natalie. Did Anna suspect Andrew?

There was George, Andrew's father. He looked unhappily at Ken when she first met him. Was there some secret there? He had an alibi.

Surely Fred wouldn't kill his own niece when she was living under his roof. Of course, there could be some dark secrets that he had which Natalie found out about, maybe something connected with Lydia. But she still didn't see any evasiveness in him during their recent discussions, and he was now accepting of her and Ken's plans to investigate. He didn't at first. Maybe his upbringing was such to let the detectives and Scotland Yard handle everything. That was a nice thought but they were failing Ken and failing Natalie.

Could it have been Dexter? He had his nose in everything. Maybe he was working on a story and thought that Natalie was going to get hers printed first. She laughed out loud at that one. Dexter just didn't seem the type to be killing a professional rival. Then she reminded herself that she had to keep an open mind and not let her attraction to him cloud her judgement. What was the extent of his relationship with Natalie? From her personal experience, she knew that Dexter was hard to resist in an emotional or a romantic way and she couldn't help thinking Dexter knew more than he was letting on.

There was Franklin, the accountant. She didn't know much about him, but noticed he was a bit nervous meeting people. He seemed reserved. Was that because he was hiding something or just because he was shy around others and did not have social skills? He was Fred's accountant and that gave him opportunity for cooking the books, as they say. She put him high on her list. Were there some accounting irregularities and how could she find out?

There was Edward, family friend and Member of Parliament. He seemed distant as well but what would his motive be? It was doubtful that in his position he would lower himself to murdering someone even if he did have a motive that was not obvious to her at the moment. He was also on her list. For some reason she suspected him but she couldn't put her finger on the reason why.

He and Franklin both had alibis.

Both Mr. and Mrs. Patel seemed nice, and poor Amanda would never hurt anyone, she'd been hurt enough. Could the murder possibly have anything to do with the relationship of Amanda and Raj? There were possibilities to consider there. Perhaps they hired someone to kill Amanda and it was a case of mistaken identity. It didn't seem likely, but she guessed Raj still had feelings for Amanda since he had not entered his arranged marriage yet.

Perhaps the Patels believed his love for Amanda was so strong that he never would honor his arranged marriage as long as Amanda was in the picture. It would be good for them to have Amanda out of the way. Or, since Natalie wrote for a society column, maybe they feared Natalie would write something about the relationship of Raj and Amanda and cause a scandal. If Natalie had taken upon herself to announce the engagement of the two, or that they were an item, the Patels would truly be scandalized and the arranged marriage would be off. Also, Mrs. Patel looked like she was hiding something so that put her high on the list of further future investigations.

Anna and Travis would have known Fred would be away, so either of them could have come back and taken her life. If they had motives, they weren't obvious. But there could be some secrets she knew about one of them, and they wanted her to be silenced. They both had strong hands – she'd seen Anna at work – and how well were their alibis checked out? She then realized this was an absurd idea, both Anna and Travis were good, honest people.

So, there it was. She was no further ahead and had a lot of investigating to do. There were so many suspects and scenarios. She could dismiss everyone she had met, or they could all be covering up and lying for each other. It seemed hopeless. Perhaps the killer would show himself or herself in due time. Or, more likely, someone would reveal something significant.

Her thoughts turned away from the murder and back again to Ken. Ah, Ken, the kindest man she had ever met. She had the faintest flashes of him holding her hand and comforting her when she was in the hospital. How much time did he spend with Jolene when he was in London while Kate was staying at the country house? He had been gone for days. Why was he kissing Jolene that night after he had indicated that he only saw Jolene as a friend? She'd had to act like she hadn't seen it, she had no right to question him about it anyway, since apparently she and Ken were just friends and comrades in an investigation. That's all they had ever been. He still seemed affectionate toward her and kissed her on the cheek in public now and then to keep up the appearance of an engagement. She could never let on that she had feelings for him beyond friendship.

In any case, she was to meet Dexter at his house later in the week. He had sent her a note. And while she did not appreciate his constant questions, she had every intention of showing up to talk with him. He seemed to have a lot of insight into the people she had met and he might perhaps provide new clues for solving Natalie's murder, whether he knew information that was relevant or not.

CHAPTER 27

The next morning, Ken and Kate talked and decided not to ask Andrew where he had purchased the exquisite marquise-cut diamond engagement ring he had bought for Natalie. They didn't want to let him know they were considering the remote possibility that he could have killed Natalie during a heated argument in which Natalie returned the ring and called off the engagement. Ken soundly rejected this idea but Kate still wondered.

Only a few jewelers in London would have sold such a rare and beautiful ring and the pair went to the most likely jeweler first, the shop where Ken had purchased the ring that Kate now was wearing.

The owner, Mr. Mason, greeted Ken with enthusiasm. He had not been at the shop when Ken and Kate were there before.

"Ken, so nice to see you again. I'm sorry I missed you last week. And who is this? I'm guessing your intended, I congratulate you."

Kate blushed slightly.

"Kate, I would like you to meet Mr. Mason. He is the finest jeweler in London and my family has done business with him for years."

"Delighted to meet you," Kate said as she extended her hand.

After shaking her hand, a concerned look came over his face. "I hope the ring is satisfactory and is the right size. Do you like it?"

"Yes, I love it. It is beautiful. Thank you for asking. It is a perfect fit."

After more small talk, Mr. Mason confirmed that he sold Andrew the ring. It was a one-of-a kind marquise-cut stone. He was clearly surprised it was missing. He said that Natalie had brought the ring in to be sized but that it had been picked up. He assumed all was well because he never heard anything to the contrary.

Ken and Kate left the store and walked back to Ken's sports car. The two looked at each other and Kate spoke first.

"What if the ring had been in Mr. Mason's store and he took the opportunity to keep it after her murder? What if he was not being honest about it being picked up?"

"Kate, really, Mr. Mason is an honorable man and would never do such a thing."

"What if he didn't know about it? What if another employee did what I just suggested, or worse case, actually murdered her? The ring must be worth thousands of pounds."

"If there was such a person, they would have had no idea that Fred was out of town or that Travis and Anna had left for the night." Ken's response was logical and Kate had to agree.

"You're right, it had to be someone who knew all that and who knew Natalie, even if we would like to believe differently. It would be comfortable and convenient to believe it was a complete stranger but I'm afraid we don't have that luxury," she said.

"Although, actually, I don't think we can totally rule out a complete stranger," Ken countered, after thinking about it for a moment. "Someone could have followed her home and assumed she was alone when she got home because the house was dark until she turned on the lights."

"That is possible," Kate agreed.

"Or, here's another thought. There had been a rash of burglaries in the area during that time. Maybe someone broke in to rob the place, thinking no one was home. Natalie may have surprised a prowler and then they panicked and killed her." Ken was throwing out anything he could think of as a possible scenario.

"Except that nothing was stolen, only some papers and her journal," Kate rationalized.

"They would have wanted to leave the scene in a hurry since the crime had become murder and didn't have a chance to take anything, except her ring which was right there on her finger, available to snatch up in a hurry. And they took the papers to confuse the police. That's possible, isn't it?"

"Yes, I suppose."

Both knew that was very unlikely. Kate had another idea.

"Mr. Mason said that the ring was picked up, but he didn't say by whom. It's a possibility that someone knew the ring was being sized and picked up the ring saying she was Natalie at a time when someone who didn't know her was working at the store."

"The only person that could be would be Jolene."

"Well, if you say so, then it could have been Jolene. I'm just thinking of reasons the ring would be missing without it being connected to the murder. Maybe we could go back to the store and ask to see the records of when the ring was picked up and if someone signed for it."

"I see what you're driving at. You think Jolene may have killed Natalie out of jealousy, don't you?" Ken was a little perturbed at Kate's insinuations. He didn't think Jolene could possibly be involved.

"No, honestly I don't. I know jealousy can lead to violence but I don't see Jolene as a killer and I can read people. My life must have depended on it during the war."

"You mean being a spy and deceiving people? Did you ever get used to the lying?"

That was a low blow and Kate looked at him with surprise in her eyes.

"I didn't consider what I was doing lying."

"What was it?"

"Playing a role. A role that needed to be played to help save England and the world from a terrible fate."

"I'm sorry. Of course, you're right. You had to do what you had to do as we all did. We all had to give up something and do things we'd prefer not to do during the war. I didn't mean anything by what I said. Please forgive me." He put his hand on her arm in a gentle way.

"I risked my life daily so that the world would be free from tyranny orchestrated by a madman. So that we could be here having this conversation."

"I know. I am quite aware of that. I, too, risked my life during the war, serving in the RAF. Again, I apologize. I guess this investigation is getting to me. You are trying to help, and I thank you, but when you voice your suspicions of my friends and family, it hurts. It's driving me mad and so I struck out at you, I'm so sorry."

"Yes, I understand completely," Kate didn't look at Ken as she said this and looked down at the ground to not reveal the disappointment she was feeling at his comments.

Ken could sense what she was feeling and said softly, "I can't do this without you, I need you, Kate."

That appeased her and she smiled. "You can count on me, we'll figure this out. And I'll try to be more delicate when I express my suspicions. Or I'll keep them to myself."

"Actually, there is something we can do to follow up on your ideas," Ken said in an accommodating tone. "I've got a photo of Natalie in my wallet. Let's see if the assistant is at the jewelry store and if he remembers her picking up the ring."

The two walked back to the store, where Mr. Mason, the owner was surprised to see them again. "Is there something else I can show you?" he asked in a friendly tone, hoping there was a chance of another sale.

"We would like to speak to your assistant, if he's here, about the ring," Ken told him.

Mason disappeared behind a velvet curtain and after a few moments a younger, well-dressed man appeared.

"Hello, my name is Charles. Mr. Mason said you'd like to speak with me. He said it's about the marquise-cut engagement ring, which I do recall," he said in a worried tone, wondering if he'd done something to offend these customers. He didn't recall seeing them before but sometimes the store got quite busy.

"This is really a long shot, but I have to ask," Ken said. "If you remember the ring, you might remember something about who picked it up after it was sized." Ken pulled out the photo of Natalie and handed it to Charles. "Her eyes were green," he said, hoping that would help him remember.

After staring intently at the photo, Charles closed his eyes. After a long while he opened them. "I've been told I have an outstanding memory," he said. "And I have never seen this woman before. I would have remembered her eyes. The woman who picked up the ring had brown eyes and dark hair."

"Thank you so much, sir," Ken said, meeting Kate's eyes for a moment. "That's all we needed to know. You have helped us solve a very important question." Ken took Kate's arm and the two walked out of the store and stood outside the shop.

"Kate, please forgive me. It's clear that Jolene took the ring. Your theory was right."

"Well at least we know what happened to the ring. It's only a small part of the mystery, though." Kate was glad Ken decided to follow up on her idea. But it didn't solve Natalie's murder, not even close.

Changing the subject to a lighter one, she said, "I'm getting hungry for lunch. I know where there's a wonderful small café nearby. Let's get our minds off murder for a while."

"Yes, that sounds very nice," he agreed. "By the way, I was wondering if any of your memory has been coming back?"

"A little. Maybe seeing some sites around London will help."

"Alright, but remember that we have to be back by 2 o'clock this afternoon. Uncle Fred is having a cocktail party on the patio."

Kate looked up at the sky. "It will be a lovely day for it. We have been blessed with wonderful weather. I wonder how long it will keep up?"

Kate did not know then that not only the weather, but her entire world would become stormy very soon.

CHAPTER 28

After a refreshing and enjoyable lunch date, Ken and Kate arrived back at the house just as the cocktail party was beginning. Fred had hired caterers to supply drinks and hors d'oeuvres, giving Anna the afternoon off. She was to return and prepare dinner in the evening. The Patel's were there so Amanda was not. Kate was disappointed because she was looking forward to seeing her. Dexter was in attendance along with Franklin. George and Edward were there with their wives. Also present were Andrew and Jolene. All suspects, thought Kate. Was it disturbing to anyone having drinks on the patio where Natalie was murdered?

Kate was served a champagne cocktail and sipped on the drink while she made small talk with Andrew's parents. They talked of the weather and the garden that Elaine Cresswell was proud of. She told Kate that Andrew was feeling much better and that playing tennis and golf with Ken was helping his recovery. George mumbled something about the ridiculous war and sauntered off to talk with the gentlemen about sporting events.

More people arrived and it was getting crowded and a bit warm on the patio so some of the guests moved into the house. A group of the women sat around the table in the dining area discussing fashions and the latest celebrity gossip.

Kate wasn't interested in their chatter and happened to notice that someone was in Fred's library as she passed by, returning from the wash room. Curious, she entered the library to find Dexter thumbing through a book he had taking down from the shelf. She closed the door behind her and they were alone.

"Well, hello Kate."

"Hi Dexter, how are you?"

"I am well, thank you. I knew Fred had some books on the Middle East and I thought I'd look something up."

"Yes, he does have an extensive library," Kate said with an engaging smile. "Oh, by the way, I would like to take you up on your invitation to come by your house tomorrow morning. I can be there at ten. Is that still good for you?"

Dexter looked puzzled for a moment. He didn't recall inviting Kate, but obviously he must have, and he was excited that she was going to come to his house. Perhaps he had mentioned her coming over one time when he had had too much to drink and forgot about it. He did have a tendency to overindulge at times. Realizing this would be an excellent opportunity, he smiled quickly and responded, "That would be splendid. Did I happen to give you the address?'

"Yes, I have it."

Nonchalantly, Dexter said, "George Cresswell was a member of a group that tried to negotiate a deal with Germany before the war. This action was illegal and he would have been arrested if he had been found out, but he disassociated himself with the group once war broke out."

Kate looked at him with a blank look on her face.

"I just thought you should know."

"Thank you. That's good to know."

Dexter looked at Kate standing next to him and looked down at the book in his hands.

"We should really talk about that kiss," he said as he closed the book and put it back on the shelf.

"What kiss? I don't remember a kiss."

"Really? Let me refresh your memory," he said as he moved close, closer to her. Again, she could smell his aftershave and feel his masculine warmth.

He leaned into Kate and kissed her passionately. Kate didn't recall ever being kissed like that before. She was taken aback at his audacity. She looked in his eyes and put her hand gently on his chest to push him away.

"This isn't right, as you know, I'm engaged to Ken."

"You've got to be kidding. Do you really think you are fooling anyone? You and Ken need to work on your acting skills. My grandmother could do a better job of pretending to be a newly engaged young woman madly in love."

"Well, I guess I don't seem very giddy."

"Who are you? Really."

Kate stared down at the floor and then looked up again into his eyes.

"To tell you the truth, Dexter, I have amnesia and I have no recollection of my past. Ken has been so kind. He has helped me to find out who I am and get back on my feet and have a life."

"So, why are you here then, posing as Ken's fiancée?"

"To help him find out who killed Natalie."

"My God."

Dexter looked in her eyes. Again, he kissed her as he put his arms around her and held her close. Now she knew what it was liked to be kissed in a way that made her feel alive, something she had only read about in romantic novels. She felt safe in his arms and was glad she could finally reveal the truth about herself. She believed she could trust him and this could possibly be the love she had been seeking.

Reason took over and she realized that people would start to miss her and at any moment, she would be caught in the arms of Dexter.

"People will wonder where I am!"

She pulled away from his embrace and ran out of the library. As she turned the corner, she ran straight into a surprised Ken. She apologized to Ken for crashing into him, smiled and walked away towards the hall and back to the patio, leaving him staring at her as she walked away.

Most of the guests were inside by now and a gentle rain was starting to fall. She could feel raindrops as she sat on the cement ledge of the patio, trying to regain her composure. She took off her sweater and wrapped it around her shoulders. Standing under the awning and watching the gentle rain, the clean refreshing smell cleared her mind and settled her soul. She could still feel Dexter's warm kisses, all of her senses aware of the taste, the scent of him.

The party was still in full swing when eventually Kate went back inside the house and joined the women in conversation. Dexter had left as had some other guests. Drinks flowed and some partygoers stayed well into the dinner hour. Anna had returned from her afternoon off and prepared a fabulous meal of roasted lamb with potatoes and greens. China, crystal and flowers adorned the dining room table. The rain began to pour with thunder and lightning crashes as the conversation carried on about business and post-war life, the weddings that were on the horizon for the servicemen home from the war and their respective brides-to-be.

Dinner was served. Kate observed that Ken and Jolene hadn't talked much together throughout the afternoon and now Kate was seated next to Ken. Jolene had strictly associated with the women in the group which was unusual for her as she normally would seek out male attention.

On the other side of Kate was seated Raj, who seemed like an intelligent, attractive and genuinely nice man. She understood why Amanda had been drawn to him and wondered if he really was planning to go along with the arranged marriage and when. When she mentioned his engagement, he clammed up, so she assumed it was not a good topic. He sparked up again as they talked about tennis as he was quite a champion on the court and this was a sport he truly loved. Kate guessed that could have been how he met Amanda, since Ken had told her that she enjoyed the sport and was a champion in her own right. It ended up being an enjoyable conversation.

The dinner was delicious, well-served and beautifully prepared. The guests raved about it and complimented Anna and their host. The wine was also excellent, vintage brought up from Fred's cellar, the perfect pairing to one of the most fabulous home-cooked meals Kate had ever tasted.

After dinner, most of the guests left, but a few stayed chatting in the sitting room. Conversation was interrupted when Dexter unexpectedly came to the door. He reeked of whiskey as he staggered in. All heads turned and everyone was stunned to see him in the condition he was in. To Kate's astonishment, he pointed to her and said loudly, "I know who you are and what you are."

The guests then turned and looked at her with question marks on their face. A few of the men led Dexter out the door, telling him he was shamefully drunk. Edward offered to drive him home, asking his wife if she could get her own ride home. Everyone else was staring at Kate. She was devastated at this performance, and felt her face turn scarlet. What could she say?

Ken rescued her again by changing the subject and engaging everyone in a new topic. Politely, they followed his lead and joined in the new conversation. Kate excused herself, embarrassed and shaken, and ran up the stairs to her room.

Lost Secrets

CHAPTER 29

The next morning, Kate awoke late since she ended up taking a sleeping draught to help her relax from the events of the day and evening before. She had been angry and hurt and it took a while to calm down. Her first thought after she sat up was that she needed to see Dexter and ask him to explain his behavior. Their planned meeting was this morning, and she wasn't going to be put off by his bad behavior.

She dressed and was applying make-up when there was a knock on the door. Thinking it might be Ken or Fred asking her to pack up and leave after last night's disaster, she gingerly opened the door. To her pleasant surprise, it was Anna, who had a concerned look on her face.

"Please come in," a relieved Kate said.

Anna entered the room and wasted no time. "On behalf of all of London, I wish to apologize for the spectacle that Dexter Flynn made of himself last night."

"Thank you," Kate whispered.

"That man! He always was annoying and bothering Natalie as well. I can honestly say I don't care for him."

This aroused Kate's attention. "Do you think his intentions toward Natalie were all professional or do you think he had a personal interest in her?"

"I think he did have a romantic interest in Natalie. I would say he lusted after her. After her death, he married another woman that he had been romantically involved with."

That bit of information surprised Kate. "Is Dexter married?"

"Not anymore."

'What happened to his wife?"

"He was away from home, stationed near the command post, covering the war and she contacted pneumonia here in London and died, very sad, with him not being there for her. Although rumor has it, she was never in very good health. A fragile woman, an artist with no interest in politics. It seemed like to everyone that it was an unusual match for him."

"Yes, it would seem that way."

"In any case, miss, he has had some bad luck but that does not condone his behavior of last night."

"I honestly have no idea what he was driving at when he said what he did." Kate's frustration was apparent as she sat on the bed. Anna sat down next to her and took her hand.

"I believe that man has delusions. Let me tell you everyone in the room was aware of him and no one took any mind to what he said," she said with a calming voice.

"Thank you again, that is very comforting."

Anna's kindness touched Kate deeply. She certainly wasn't going to tell her that her intention was to visit Dexter in a few hours.

"Come down to the kitchen and I will make you some breakfast."

"That's kind of you, although I think just toast and tea this morning. I would like to do some shopping today," Kate said looking away. She could not look Anna in the eye and lie to her about her plans for the morning. Looking at her watch, she gasped, seeing that it was almost nine and she told Dexter she would arrive about ten.

"Has Ken already had breakfast?"

"Yes, he has eaten and left. I don't know where he went, he didn't say."

CHAPTER 30

Dexter awoke with a start, ten minutes before his alarm bell was set to go off. It must have been the bad dream he was having, something about men with guns chasing him through darkened streets and weird clown figures popping up whenever he thought he was gaining ground on them. A bit of shell-shock left over from his participation in and journalistic coverage of the war. He had been sent to the front lines and what he witnessed still haunted him.

Shaking it off, he showered, dressed and looked in the mirror. The bright silk yellow handkerchief he tucked into his suitcoat pocket was in memory of his wife. She had been loving and kind, although never in good health. He felt blessed to have spent four wonderful years with her at his side before she died from pneumonia. It was a sad memory that he had been working as a war correspondent when she passed. Sheila had been a painter and enjoyed brilliant colors. Now he always made sure to wear bright color somewhere on his person to show his respect.

Kate entered his thoughts. He was surprised she had attracted his attention so strongly. There was something about her, some undefined pull he felt towards her. Maybe he could help her remember her past. If she had been an allied operative behind enemy lines, he could write some sensational stories for the paper, not mentioning her name, of course. He would keep her as his surreptitious source. And if they became a couple, better yet. What amazing experiences might she relay to him? And more importantly, how could he win her affections?

He kept running into her, at the library and at parties. Maybe she was starting to have feelings for him. He knew the time he kissed her on an impulse during the after-wedding party was a bit out-of-line and premature. He should have waited until there was more time to make his intentions known to her, after realizing her engagement to Ken was a sham. He thought about her almost constantly, much to his dismay. And in the library at Fred's house she had kissed him back and confided in him so maybe there was hope of a relationship.

Today was the day she had agreed to meet with him at his house. She had said she would be arriving at ten and that she would take a taxi there and not bother Fred's driver. Therefore, she was coming alone. He had nothing against Ken, but of course, saw him as a potential romantic rival. What exactly was their relationship? Surely, he didn't bring her to London just to investigate his sister's murder. He must have some feelings for her.

Last night, though, was pretty awful. He had gone to a pub and was well past his usual 3-drink limit. He remembered going to Fred Michael's house and making accusations at Kate, frustrated that she kept pushing him away and giving him mixed messages. He also wanted to tell her what he had found out from Mr. Robertson. He had called Robertson after leaving the cocktail party to find out more about Kate (since Robertson seemed to recognize her at the library) with the plan of revealing to her what he had found out. But that certainly was not the way to do it. Hopefully Kate would forgive him. He didn't remember much about what he'd said but hoped she'd still come over and talk, give him a chance to properly apologize. He would be a perfect gentleman and show her that side of him. This was his one great opportunity to catch her alone and finally make his intentions known, no more games.

And what would he reveal to her? Clearly, he had aroused her curiosity. He'd been working on an extremely delicate story, on his own since the paper hadn't given him permission to write this once-in-a lifetime article he had started. A German spy ring that had flourished unnoticed in Worcestershire. As if Natalie was helping him from beyond the grave, he happened to find a key she had given him a week before her death to a safety deposit box. It was hidden inside a cigar case she had given him for a present and he never thought to open it. He found it yesterday as he was cleaning up his house in anticipation for his lovely guest due to arrive this morning. At his first opportunity, he would go to the bank and open the box. In it, he supposed, would be valuable information. There had to be some important reason Natalie wanted him to have it.

After a breakfast of eggs, kippers, toast and tea, he sat in his favorite chair. Sipping his second cup of tea, he decided she would be at his house soon. He picked up the daily post and began to read.

At about 9:45 a knock sounded on his door. He was startled from reading an intense story on how the munitions development was going in America and how Britain and America had become the best of allies.

So she had come early, what a surprise. He opened the door with a smile on his face and was greeted by a familiar face pointing a large gun at him. Backing up and in shock, he said "What on earth are you doing here?" These were the last words he spoke as Dexter was blasted by a luger back into his entryway, blood spattering on the walls. As quickly and stealthily as the killer had come to Dexter's door, the assassin laid the gun next to Dexter's body, took off dark leather gloves and disappeared onto the street, blending in with others, anonymous. All was silent in Dexter's house as blood seeped from his chest wound and darkened the white carpet.

Kate arrived, breathless, at 10:05. Raising her fingers to knock, she saw the door was slightly ajar. She pushed it in and stepped into the entryway. The sight that greeted her was appalling and her thoughts immediately flashed back to a similar scene from years ago. She had come through the front door of her parents' house and found them laying in blood on the floor. Anger and shock arose in her throat like a huge eagle and she saw the gun lying on the floor near Dexter's body. She could hear a sound coming from the bedroom. Without thinking, she picked up the gun and began searching through the rest of the house to see if the murderer was lurking about. As she entered the bedroom, she saw a sleek small black cat that had jumped from the dresser down to the floor and stared at her helplessly. Kate walked back to the front of the house. Just then two men in police uniforms came barging through the open door and stared at her, as she stood in the hallway with a gun in her hand and Dexter's body on the ground.

"Put down the gun, miss, and put your hands in the air, we're not here to harm you," the more rotund of the policemen said, as he gave a sideways look to his partner. She didn't respond. "It's okay, it's over, please just lay the gun down and let us talk with you a bit." He used a gentle voice with the hope she would respond to reason, although he suspected she was not in her right mind. He was fearful this might be his last day on earth.

To his amazement, she gently lay the gun down on the floor, her hands in the air. Her eyes staring but not seeing anything. The two policemen looked at each other and shook their heads. The younger, thinner one found Dexter's telephone and called for an ambulance and reinforcements. It looked like they had caught the murderer red-handed and she seemed like a looney-cake.

The next thing Kate knew, she was in an empty cell with only a toilet and a cot. How could this have happened? A million thoughts ran through her head as she tried to process it. *Why Dexter? Why dear Dexter? And what trouble am I in?*

CHAPTER 31

The next morning Kate was sitting on the flat hard bunk in her cell, her head in her hands, when the prim and proper uniformed female guard opened the door and motioned for her to follow. The woman wouldn't smile or respond to any of her questions. Kate had no choice but to follow her. She inhaled deeply as she walked out into the hall, relieved to be out of the stale and claustrophobic cell in which she had spent the night. She had gotten at most an hour's sleep, the blanket was thin, the room was cold and there were constant clanging and banging noises along with any number of varied voices speaking, which were not quite loud enough to make head or tails of.

They walked down a number of corridors and closed doors, past a sign that said "Interrogation," where the woman directed her into a room which contained a tape recorder and a table and several chairs. Kate could see a black screen on one side of the room, probably an observation mirror, she thought. Sitting down with her hands folded on the table, she tried not to gasp in surprise when Mr. Robertson walked in the door.

"Hello Miss Richter. You are probably wondering who I am and why I'm here and seem to know you," Robertson said, sitting down and producing a new box of cigarettes, which he absent-mindedly opened as he spoke.

"Yes sir, please fill me in."

He took and lit a cigarette, offering Kate one which she declined. "My name is Ryan Robertson and I'm been following you to see if you were who I thought you were."

"And?"

"Yes, I believe you are. Has any of your memory come back?"

Kate's eyes grew wide and she gasped slightly. "Could you tell me who you believe I am, and what is this talk about my memory?"

"Dexter Flynn called me Saturday afternoon to talk about you. He told me you had amnesia, which explained a lot to me. I always wondered why you didn't acknowledge me or even seem to recognize me."

"Dexter called you?"

"Yes, he wanted to find out if I knew anything about you so that he could be the one to tell you about your past."

"Really?" Kate was pleasantly surprised. "He must have truly cared about me."

"I've also been talking to Kenneth Michaels."

"I see. I was hoping that Ken would visit me here."

"I decided it was best to talk to you alone. Mr. Michaels has been here, he is supportive of you and tried to see you when you were in your cell but was not allowed."

It was comforting to Kate to know that Ken had attempted to see her. Kate wondered when they would discuss Dexter's murder. She knew that was why she had been jailed and was anxious to be given a chance to defend herself and explain the circumstances of why she was at his house when she was arrested. Robertson was supposedly a government agent, but there must be a reason why he was questioning her in this room. What was he up to? She decided to make the first move.

"I know it looked very bad when the policemen came to Dexter's house, but I didn't kill him."

Robertson took a drag on his cigarette, looked at Kate, but did not say anything. He had an impassive air about him and Kate had no idea what the man's intentions or thoughts were.

"Let's talk more about you first, then we'll get to that.," he said after a few seconds of silence.

"Alright, that will be fine. Did Ken tell you how we met?"

Robertson flicked his cigarette ashes into the ashtray on the desk. "Yes, he told me the incredible story. We always wondered what happened to you. We assumed you were found out and killed. That's why I was surprised and elated when I saw you in London. When I was meeting with Dexter in the library I asked him if he knew your name and he told me. You can't imagine how happy I was to find out that you made it out of Germany alive and well. We thought you were lost. The lost spy."

Kate was not clear on what he was getting at. Who was this "we" he was mentioning? She looked at him and said, slowly, "I've had flashes of previous events in my life since I've been back in London, but not even close to a normal person's recollections."

"Do you remember that you were a member of a select group working in an effort called Operation Double-Cross, to convince the Nazi's that the invasion into France by the Allies was to be at Calais and not Normandy? I was one of the architects of that group."

"I did piece together that I must have been an allied agent. I didn't know what my assignment was and I didn't realize you.....I'm pleased to meet you, I'm sure, Mr. Robertson. Or, I guess, see you again."

"As I am to see you. I know these are not the best of circumstances, but since you're here I'm able to finish up the business I've been assigned. Miss Richter, I've been authorized to give you an accommodation from the crown for your participation in that operation. I have a medal for you, with the thanks of a grateful nation. It's called the Medal of Honor."

Kate was overcome with relief and joy. She now knew that the authorities knew who she was, so perhaps they might realize that she wasn't likely to murder Dexter. She hoped that her past would have earned her some trustworthiness and personal capital and they would be willing to hear her story.

"You were an allied spy in Germany and helped win the war, we want to thank you."

"Thank you, Mr. Robertson, I appreciate that, very much."

He looked at Kate and asked, "Were you ever afraid? Do you remember?"

"No, I don't remember fear. I'm sure I had full confidence in the British spy network, more so as time went by. I don't consider myself a hero, or at least not to the extent of the people that openly defied the Nazis. I have done a lot of reading since I've been here. I've read about those who resisted being shot or imprisoned for speaking up. I remember my dear parents were killed, most likely for the same reason."

There was a moment of subdued silence. They could hear the clock ticking on the wall.

Kate continued, "Even though I made a contribution to the allied war effort, reading about these others has made me very humble. The Jewish resistance in the Warsaw ghetto that was brutally smashed, those were real brave souls. The Nazi's that I was infiltrating with bad Intel were more than willing to believe that I actually was on their side and supported their brutality and insanity. The only way I could stand to be in the same room with them was that I knew I was working against them in every way I could. I do remember that."

Robertson looked at Kate with admiration. He had no doubt that this woman was honest and sincere.

"And now Dexter Flynn has been murdered so it seems to never end," Kate said, almost in a whisper.

"Do you have any idea who might have murdered him? Please tell me everything you know."

"I received a note from him to meet him at his home at 10 o'clock yesterday morning. The note lured me in by saying he had some information I would be interested in. He pleaded with me to meet him. Unfortunately, I destroyed the note. I realize now it could be valuable evidence."

"That is very unfortunate. Please go on."

"When I arrived, I was a little late and arrived about 10:05, I saw him lying in a pool of blood."

Kate placed her fingers on her cheek as she considered something she now found very strange. She looked at Robertson and said, "Now that I think about it, he seemed puzzled when I told him that I was responding to his invitation. He acted like he didn't remember asking me to his house but then quickly said he was looking forward to my visit. It must have been a set-up. Someone else must have sent me that note. I walked right into the killer's trap to murder Dexter and frame me."

"What did you do when you came into his house and found him dead?"

"I heard a noise in the other room so I picked up the gun that was lying next to him and went to search to see if the killer was still about. I wanted the gun with me, just in case. It was my first reaction and a stupid one. I was reacting out of shock and fear. When I investigated, it was his cat. She had jumped down from his dresser. I realize it looked very bad that they found me holding the gun. Someone must have called the police."

"Yes, it was an anonymous tip, most likely from the assassin."

"Have you been able to trace the gun?"

"No, it was a military issue. It was never privately owned and can't be traced. The assassin must have left it there to incriminate you, knowing that you would have access to such a weapon. Both Fred and Ken were in the service and have them, I'm sure."

"Yes, they do. I've seen them locked in a case in a room at the back of the house."

A silent pause ensued as Kate looked down at the floor, feeling a current of emotional pain.

"Do you know . . . did anyone take on the cat?"

A smile came over his face, "Dexter had an older sister, she was notified yesterday right after your arrest." Robertson was pleased that Kate felt concern for the animal. "She will adopt the cat and take care of his affairs. She is grief stricken, as you can well imagine, but she has a supportive husband and two grown children."

"I'm glad he has family to handle things after his passing." Kate was relieved to hear about the cat, it was a minor detail but it had bothered her, not knowing what would happen to it.

"Do you have any idea who might have wished him harm?"

"Maybe you could tell me. When you were meeting with him at the library, did he say what was he working on? It might be connected to some story he was investigating."

"He arranged the meeting with me to ask questions about spy operations during the war. Of course most information is classified and I couldn't answer his questions, even if I wanted to. He was asking about a spy-ring Natalie Michaels had mentioned to him. Do you know - were he and Natalie close?"

"Yes, I believe they were very close. They worked together."

"Did Dexter tell you anything else that might help with the investigation?"

"He told me there was an organization in England set up to undermine the war effort. These people were negotiating with Nazi Germany in an unofficial and illegal capacity."

Robertson smiled slightly, "Yes, I was aware of these misguided people. They must now realize how wrong they were."

"Indeed."

"That story was closed a long time ago so I doubt if that was what he was working on."

"I wonder why he mentioned it to me then. Maybe he thought that group had something to do with Natalie's murder."

They both looked down, deep in thought about the disastrous events that had taken place during the war, the bombings, the killings, the rationing, the lies and the fear that Germany could not be beaten.

The conversation then turned back to the matter at hand as Robertson said, "I need to know more about your relationship with Dexter. We interviewed Sir Frederick Michaels and he told us about the scene Saturday night when Dexter came barging into his house and what he had said to you. Can you explain why he may have said what he did?"

"I honestly don't know. I've been going over it in my head. Maybe he thought I was leading him on romantically and that I was a tease. Especially now that I assume he didn't actually invite me to his house but I told him I would be coming over. I can see why he was confused, I was inadvertently giving him mixed signals. I constantly submitted to him and then pushed him away."

Kate looked at Robertson to see if he had any reaction, possibly judging her indiscretion. Not seeing anything, she continued, "Or perhaps he wanted to tell me what he found out from you. I didn't realize he called you that afternoon. I was going to ask him to explain himself during my visit. He was quite drunk when he came to Fred's house that night."

"Sir Fred also mentioned that you were seen kissing Dexter outside on the terrace at a party. And of course, you know how people gossip."

So, Fred ratted me out. Oh well, I suppose I can't blame him.

"Oh, dear God, yes I can see what people might conclude if I am charged. The first time I met him was at Ken's cousin's wedding, then I saw him at the library the day that he was with you, and then at an after-wedding party at the Ness hotel. He did steal a kiss at that party. He asked me to join him outside on the terrace to have a chat. I was surprised but didn't think much of it, chalking it up the party atmosphere. It was a flirtation, nothing more. I should have realized that someone would have seen us together. Again, I saw him at Fred's house Saturday. He left the party and later that night was the scene when he came back to the house intoxicated."

She took a deep breath and continued, "We had a friendly relationship although he at times did seem to want more than that. I admired him and I admit I was strongly attracted to him, as most women were, I imagine. He was quite handsome. I was beginning to have feelings for him and I can't believe he's gone. The world has lost not only an important and wonderful journalist, but a fine man." The sadness on Kate's face was unmistakable. Robertson had interviewed a lot of suspects in his career and he could tell that she was grieving for this man.

This was the first time she'd been able to talk freely about herself, and the words came tumbling out in spite of herself. "Mr. Robertson, I've led a sheltered life and the idea of some male romantic attention did prove very enticing to me. I'm afraid I was succumbing to his romantic overtures. Ken seemed to be falling for a friend of the family, Jolene. Perhaps I was feeling left out. I had come to London with the ruse of being Ken's fiancée to help him investigate the murder of his sister, Natalie. I should have resisted Dexter's attention and I am embarrassed to admit that a lot of my indiscretion with Dexter was due to Ken's apparently close relationship to Jolene. I also thought Dexter might have had clues about Natalie's murder, whether he knew it or not. As I've said, that's why I went to his house. Of course, I was also expecting an apology for his outburst at the house and an explanation of why he chose to confront me in that way."

Robertson told her that he believed in her innocence and that Scotland Yard was on her side as well, knowing of the risks she took during the war to help the Allies and the lack of motive on her part to commit the crime. They also came to the conclusion that it was a set-up and they convinced the local authorities.

"I've talked to the authorities and you will not be charged. You will be released this morning but I must tell you, I believe that you are in danger. Whoever killed Dexter tried to frame you for his murder so he or she will continue to see you as a threat. They will be disappointed that you have been set free and perhaps will become desperate. Obviously, they sent you the note to meet with Dexter at his house and phoned in that anonymous tip after the murder. I would advise you to stop investigating the murder of Natalie Michaels and let Scotland Yard handle the investigation. You can share with Detective Spencer what your thoughts are regarding the murder and what you have found out. He will be in touch with you shortly."

What a relief!

"You can go back to Sir Frederick's house. He and Ken are waiting for your return. However, please don't leave London without letting us know your whereabouts."

"Thank you very much, Mr. Robertson. I'm anxious to go back to the house and freshen up."

"I'll stop by Sir Fred's house later and fill them in. I'll bring the medal we want to give you with me."

Robertson realized that Kate probably did not get any sleep the last night and was feeling tired and not as alert as she usually was. "Please remain in this room, an officer will come to release you."

"Thank you for your help. And thank you for the medal, I am honored and will cherish it."

The shock of Dexter's demise, the night in jail, and the meeting with Mr. Robertson brought more of Kate's memory back. She had to admit to herself that she would rather forget some things about her past. Regardless, memories did come flooding back as she sat there alone at the table, waiting to be released.

CHAPTER 32

Kate's memories - June 12, 1939

Kate was not surprised when she received the letter. It was in a plain white envelope with no return address. She opened it with trepidation, not sure what to expect. After reading it twice, she set it down on the table and closed her eyes for a moment. Apparently, it had not gone unnoticed that she was at the top of her class at the university she attended. She had majored in Economics, a topic that had always interested her. She also was fluent in French and, of course, German since she was a German citizen.

The letter was from MI5. Kate realized that most likely a spy network was being put in place to prepare for what looked like an impending war with Germany. She assumed this was a call to support her new homeland in the counter-intelligence arena. The letter requested her presence at the British Embassy on June 14, 1939.

She was on time for the meeting and was escorted to a waiting area on the third floor. Her name was called after a few minutes and she was brought to a small office where a large man was standing behind a dark oak desk. He was dressed in an expensive pinstripe suit and she could tell he was a very important person.

"Greetings young lady, please sit down," he said as he motioned her to a chair across from his desk. His booming voice matched his size. "No doubt you are wondering why we've called you here."

"Yes, your letter was rather cryptic, but I am hoping I can be of service to you." She sat with her purse in her lap. She had worn her best suit, low heels, a small hat, with her hair tied back. She tried to sound very confident.

"If you decide to work with us, you will be facing many dangers." He cleared his throat and continued. "We have investigated your background thoroughly and believe you support Britain in what looks like a looming problem with Germany. Is this true?"

"Yes, sir. Although I was born in Germany I have been schooled here and my parents were brutally murdered in Germany. If you have done research on me, you will know that they were murdered in Berlin because of speaking out against the horrible things that were going on there, the rise of the Nazi party. I can assure you, I am appalled by the leader, Adolph Hitler and all that he stands for. His actions will destroy Germany, the Germany that I used to love. I believe his sanity is questionable."

"Such strong words coming from such a pretty woman," the man commented. "Your loyalty is of grave importance to us. Because you speak fluent German and French, and if you are willing to support the British cause, we are asking you to risk your life."

"I was anticipating this meeting and I have thought things over the last two days and have come to realize that I want to avenge the deaths of my parents and help my British countrymen. I will go anywhere you ask and do anything you want me to do. I am willing to risk my life for this cause."

Financial and logistical agreements were reached and Kate started her career as an operative in Berlin for MI5. Her shorthand, her fluent French and English and her typing skills were more than adequate qualifications for a secretarial position in the German Intelligence service.

She arrived in Germany within three weeks, traveling first by boat to France, then taking trains to Berlin. She was given a German passport and registration papers and a new name, Katherine Wolfe. The new name was given so that no one would connect her to her parents. A small apartment was prepared for her and she was assigned to work for German Intelligence for a man by the name of Helmet Mueller. She was told that a man at the top of German Intelligence was at odds with the Nazis. This is why they were able to arrange her position there without arousing suspicion.

Kate knew she was just a cog in the wheel, a small part of the larger operation to stop the Germans from their evil plans. She did not know that the Allied effort would turn the course of the war and that British Intelligence would astound the world and prevail in their efforts to crush the Axis or, that by 1944, all of the German spies in Britain would be captured or turned.

She felt fortunate to survive each day, worried about being found out and the toll on her stress level was high, but she was determined. She was lonely but had to be careful not to get too close to anyone in case they might learn her secrets. Several men had flirted with her; to keep them away she said she was engaged and that her intended was in the military. It would not do to have a man following her around. She spoke German all the time but longed to return back to England, knowing she somehow would once the war was over, if she survived.

Inside the pretty heart locket necklace she wore was an L-pill. This was the lethal suicide pill she would swallow were she ever caught, to avoid putting other operatives at risk. She never hesitated in her vow to avenge the death of her parents. She was also given a small pistol that would fit in her pocket or purse. She was trained to prepare for the worst.

Her assignment was to pass on false information to German intelligence, and covertly pass correct information on to London. It was very hard for her to outwardly proclaim loyalty to Hitler and the Third Reich while inside feeling hatred toward those who complacently followed such unethical leadership.

Time passed; the Americans joined the war, Italy had turned its back on Hitler, who was fighting wars on both fronts. The American and British forces took over part of France and Italy and were advancing inland. Kate helped to supply the intelligence that led the Germans to believe that the allied invasion would be at Calais where the Germans were prepared and not Normandy, which was being held by inexperienced young soldiers unprepared for an invasion of the size that they faced.

She'd been working in Berlin for close to five years when, on a Tuesday, her superior, Herr Mueller, summoned her to the back room of the office. She had long ago realized that Mueller was a secret anti-Nazi plotter and was now working for the British.

"Kate, London has an urgent need for more field operatives. Are you interested in leaving Berlin and working more closely to the front, where RAF paratroopers are landing? We could use your help."

"I will do whatever I can to help. I'm certainly ready for a change."

CHAPTER 33

Hamminkeln, Germany, March 15, 1945

The Rhine River was an important tool for the Germans to transport supplies, and it created a boundary behind which they were operating in the later stages of the war. The town of Wesel, situated on the east side of the River, had been an industrial hub supporting the German Army effort. However, it was bombarded from Allied raids and was suffering greatly, with nearly all of the city in ruins. It was also a strategic location that Field Marshal Montgomery, who was commander of the Allied troops, wanted to capture to clear the Diersfordt forest of its German forces, and take over three bridges crossing the river.

A few miles north was the village of Hamminkeln. The small hamlet consisted mostly of housing for workers who traveled every day to Wesel, and it also held the German Army Command Post for the area. Staffed with uprooted officers from Berlin, the post was used mainly for communication purposes, as Hitler had reduced the number of foot soldiers in the area, and there was little air support left.

Allied forces were making headway on taking back Germany. They rallied under Montgomery for Operation Plunder, a strategic operation with the goal of using the Allied American and RAF troops to enter Northern Germany. The plan was to land two airborne paratroop divisions in this area to secure the bridges, capture the towns, to be followed by ground forces who would clear the area of German forces and march onward across the Rhine River, heading always towards Berlin.

Hitler at the time was feeling pressure on all sides as his Third Reich was faltering. He was unaware of the planned attack and was struggling to stay afloat with his troops spread across all of his borders. It was after D-Day and within two months it would be reported that he committed suicide as he saw his maneuvers crumble and fail.

Kate was stationed in an apartment on the outskirts of Hamminkeln, working as a secretary for Commandant Steinhelm at the German Command Post. Steinhelm was a lazy man, preferring to let his underlings do most of the work. He left it to Kate to create and transmit his status letters to Hitler and file his reports. It was easy for her to "adjust" the information he was sending and receiving. She was provided with much of the data to use from a number of contacts the British had planted or were working with, within the German Army. Steinhelm trusted her implicitly, had no reason to doubt her allegiance. She had a nice smile and was pretty to look at. She seemed so efficient as well and had come highly recommended. She used her translation skills to help him understand the many pieces of correspondence that went through the post on a daily basis.

A recent outside contact whom Kate was instructed by MI5 to consult with during late-night hours was Kenneth Michaels, a Major in the RAF 6th Airborne Division. He had parachuted into the area a week earlier, and was in charge of preparing the way for his men, who were going to be dropped from planes on the 16th to work on securing several bridges. She found him quite attractive, with a solid conscience, a strong dedication, and a sense of humor.

Michaels met her at a house several doors down from her residence. The family living there had secretly been supporting the Allies, and were doing all they could to help the British and American forces. Kate was extremely careful as she crept out the back window of her first-floor apartment and made her way to their rendezvous. Michaels would give her a written document, which she would memorize, and then would burn it and place the ashes in the fireplace. Their encounters were brief, but the high point of her day. He didn't even know her name; that was part of the plan. In case anyone was captured, the identity of agents would be protected.

On their third meeting, he told her that he and his men were going to be stationed at Schnappenberg the next day, as a major operation was moving forward.

"It's been nice working with you," he said. "This bloody war is hell, and we probably won't ever meet again. I don't know anything about you, but I wish you well. I want you to know that I have confidence the allied troops will eventually conquer Hitler and his minions and make the world safe again."

"I'm hopeful as well. It's good to know there are capable men in the forces like you." She felt embarrassed after saying this and turned a slight shade of pink.

"We do what we have to do, don't we?" Michaels asked, and looked down. She knew this was her cue to leave and did so.

After returning to her apartment, she felt a pang of sadness, knowing there would be losses of men during the upcoming battles, and hoped that Michaels would make it through alive. It was hard being only one small part of the British Intelligence wheel, unsure of whether or not her efforts were really making a difference. Major Michaels lived in England. Maybe someday there would be peace and she could return to England and look him up. Would he remember her?

Lost Secrets

CHAPTER 34

Hamminkeln, Germany, March 16, 1945

After arriving at work the next day promptly at eight., Kate checked the incoming dispatches for Steinhelm as she usually did. She had gone through three of them when suddenly she gasped. Somehow the Germans had found out about the plans to secure the bridge Michaels had mentioned, and an air raid was planned at the very location he and his men were moving to.

Good God, would this war ever end? Was there anything she could do? A million ideas were going through her mind, all sorts of options and traps and bad endings and a glimmer of hope. She sat down and took a deep breath, and came up with a plan. First of all, she would tell Steinhelm she felt ill and had to go home. She hadn't missed a day of work yet and she'd been there for months. Then, she'd have to figure out a way to warn Michaels. Fear or delay was not an option and she took action.

Her bicycle was her only means of transportation. She had no way of knowing which direction his troops would be heading, but figured they'd be taking the quickest route, through the forest for cover. They probably started moving last night under cover of darkness. Putting on a sweater and long skirt, she looked in the mirror. She tied her hair back and covered it with an old scarf. Most of her clothes were second-hand and the sweater was large for her. She packed a bag with a few toiletries and a raincoat in case of rain. She strapped a basket with produce on top of her bike so it would look like she was returning from the market. She hopped on her bike and pedaled toward the path she suspected the troops would take through the forest.

She pedaled for miles, with her legs aching and her arms cramping from being in the same position for so long. As she neared the bridge Michaels had mentioned, she put on the brake and stopped, listening and looking around her. Off in the distance to her right, she saw some lights and movement toward the edge of the forest. If she'd been stationing a group of men, that's where she'd organize them.

Leaning her bike next to a tree, she began walking toward the movement, keeping under cover as best she could, walking through the trees. As she came closer she could see it was an encampment of men in uniforms. Thank goodness they weren't German! Now, how to find Michaels. She would just have to be persistent.

Walking up to some men at the edge of the camp, she said in English, "I need to talk with Major Michaels, it's urgent."

The men laughed and said, "Why would you need to talk with him? You can talk with us instead."

"Because I have Intel for him from British Command and it is extremely important."

She stared at the men and they stared back and finally they decided she might be telling the truth. In any case, it would be up to the Major to decide what to do with her.

"Good Grief! What are you doing here?" Michaels was distressed to see her, as there was so much to do and a woman in their midst wasn't going to help.

"I came to warn you that the Germans know where you are and are going to bomb your group. I read it in a dispatch this morning and rode my bike here as quickly as I could."

"How could they know? This mission is top secret."

"I don't know, but I strongly suggest you move your men as soon as possible to another area."

Michaels considered what Kate had said and decided to heed her warning. She probably had more up-to-date Intel than he, she being in direct contact and he being in the field. Immediately he summoned his second-in-command and started taking actions toward moving his men. Kate watched in amazement as he handled all of the details, directing this group and that group. She felt like she was finally doing something to help, something she could actually see right before her eyes.

Michaels instructed Kate to stay in his tent, and said they would be the last to leave, after he had ensured his men were moved to a safer area. She waited for what seemed like hours, and he finally returned.

"Alright, my men have been moved to a different area. What are you going to do now? Do you have the strength to pedal all that way back to where you live? It looks like it will be dark before you get home." Michaels was businesslike and rational but inside he hated to see her go, especially knowing it would be dark long before she arrived home.

"Yes, I do have the strength and it would be best if I returned to my apartment before I'm missed. I have a light on my bike so I'll be alright in the dark."

She turned to go but as she started to leave, Ken stopped her, turned her around to face him, took her hand gently and looked in her eyes, "I don't even know your name. I know it's not protocol but...."

Kate brushed up against his face and whispered in his ear, "My name is Kate."

Just then a loud whirring noise swept over their heads and there were flashes of light and loud explosions. One of the bombs hit the far side of their tent and Kate and Michaels were thrown to the ground. Michaels picked himself up, bruised and with a few cuts. Kate was closer to where it hit and she lay there, unconscious. He tried to wake her up but she didn't respond. He could tell she had a concussion caused by the blow to her head and the percussion of the blast. She had hit the ground hard. Her face had a laceration from the glass from the window that was shattered. She was bleeding! Taking a bandage from a first-aid kit he had, he placed one over the wound. The planes moved on and it became quiet again. Thank God for this woman alerting him to this. His men had avoided the attack, the main bombing had occurred exactly where his troops had been. This last bomb was on the outer edge of the area and only he and Kate were hit. The men were safe, thanks to her.

He looked at her and considered what to do in this unforeseen predicament, knowing he couldn't just leave her there to bleed to death and considered what action to take. Then he came up with an idea. He searched her pockets for identification but found none. He took out Natalie's passport and put it in her pocket. Then he looked at the locket necklace around Kate's neck and knew that it wouldn't do. He took it off and replaced it with Natalie's gold locket necklace.

Not much time passed before his radio crackled. Apparently it had survived the blast. "Michaels, do any of your men need medical assistance? We've got a plane ready to pick up the wounded."

He responded quickly. "Yes, there is a woman who is unconscious. She needs to be returned to England immediately."

CHAPTER 35

Back at Fred's house, July 1945

Fred and Ken were enjoying a cup of tea in the parlor when Travis informed them that someone was at the door. He didn't say who, just motioned them in the direction of the hallway. The two stood up and were surprised to see Kate walking in through the doorway.

"Kate!" Ken exclaimed. Their initial surprise wore off quickly and Ken hurried toward her. She could see questions in both of their eyes.

"They've released you," Ken said, stating the obvious as he put his arms around her in huge bear hug. She hugged him back, then pulled away and looked him straight in the eyes. He seemed relieved to see her. Good, she thought, maybe he did still care about her. God knows what he must have thought when she was found at a murder scene with a gun in her hand.

"Fred and I hired the best barrister in all of London for you."

Kate smiled and said softly, "How strange that sounds, a barrister for me. But it's my understanding that won't be necessary. Mr. Robertson from MI5 has spoken with the authorities and I will not be formally charged or tried for murder. Mr. Robertson will explain everything to you. He said he would stop by later." She sat down in one of the leather chairs. The two men sat down as well, both looking at her with question marks.

Ken reached out and took her hand. "Mr. Robertson came by yesterday afternoon and told Fred and me that you were at the station, and what had happened to Dexter. Anna wasn't here so she doesn't know anything about it. As you can imagine, we were incredibly concerned. He asked us a few questions about Dexter and you and then he left. Robertson told me not to worry, but I've been a basket-case."

"Thanks for your worry, Ken. It was a long night."

"I'm so glad you've been released. I tried to come in and see you but they wouldn't let me. Robertson will vouch for my unwavering support of you during this time. They told me to come back tomorrow, but here you are!"

"Yes, Kate, I've been worried about you as well," Fred said, although he didn't seem quite as sincere as Ken.

With a warm smile, Kate said, "Robertson did tell me that you came to try to see me. Ken, I'm glad they wouldn't let you come in. It wasn't a very nice place. I shouldn't have liked you to visit." She gently released his hand. "Thanks for trying, though. It means a lot to me."

Her night in the prison cell had jaded her sense of well-being. It had been a nightmare, remembering seeing Dexter's white face and the blood, and the Bobbies looking at her as if she were a crazed killer. Things had appeared stacked against her, she imagined a sham trial. She didn't know if she would ever see Ken again, and there were so many things she wanted to say to him.

"Kate, you must be famished. Would you like something to eat? It's Anna's day off but I can make you anything you would like, eggs, toast, anything."

"Perhaps some tea."

"Coming right up."

Kate excused herself to visit the bathroom. After splashing her face with warm water and drying it on clean, plush towels on the towel rack by the sink, she returned to the sitting room and sat down on the sofa. It wasn't long before Ken brought in the tea pot and a cup. She helped herself to a soothing cup of tea.

No one spoke as she sipped from her cup, each quietly pondering the situation.

"Would you like anything else, Kate?" Ken asked.

"Thank you, no. I'm very tired. I didn't sleep well. If you don't mind, I would like to freshen up and rest for a while." Her voice reflected how weary she felt

Ken finally noticed how pale she appeared and the dark circles around her eyes. "Of course, dear," he said and looked at Fred, who nodded in agreement. "Please take all the time you need and if you want for anything, just ask."

"I'll see you later then." Kate gingerly gave Ken and Fred each a brief hug and walked upstairs to her room.

Laying on the bed, she mused a bit at what had just happened. Ken seemed sincerely concerned about her. But Fred had seemed surprised to see her out of prison. Did Fred have doubts about her innocence? Being in his position, she figured he could easily have suspicions that she killed Dexter. He also might be upset that she had brought scandal to his house, reasonably so. Murder was one thing, romantic scandal quite another. Or did he know something? She was too tired to think anymore and after taking off her clothes she'd worn for two days – which she swore never to wear again – she slipped into her nightgown. She climbed into bed, between the sheets and fell fast asleep.

Within the hour, Robertson arrived and spoke with Ken and Fred. He told them everything, the entire conversation with Kate, her commendation from the crown. He handed Ken the war medal which he gratefully accepted on Kate's behalf. Fred was completely taken aback at the story of how Ken and Kate met, what she had been involved in and that their relationship was a ruse to investigate the murder of Natalie. His response was a mixture of admiration, shock and slight anger at all he was hearing. How could they have been involved in something so extraordinary? Why had he been left in the dark about all of this until now? Didn't they trust his discretion? That was the most upsetting part – not being told the truth all this time.

Robertson asked Kenneth that they no longer try to solve the murder of Natalie and leave it to Scotland Yard. Ken agreed it was possible their investigations could have led to Dexter's murder and the attempt to frame Kate for it. Ken said he'd step aside to let the most capable Detective Spencer take over. He suggested that they meet with Spencer to compare notes, and after that, he and Kate would enjoy London and carry on a normal existence.

But even while he was reassuring Robertson, Ken resolved to find out who was responsible for these murders. This evil person had gone after two women he cared for and he wasn't about to let it rest.

Right after Mr. Robertson left, Ken searched for his car keys and told Fred he was going to see Detective Spencer. Fred watched his determined nephew say goodbye and walk through the door.

****

"And what brings you here today, Mr. Michaels?" the detective asked.

"I want your personal assurance that Kate is not going to be charged for Dexter's murder."

"She will not, that's the word from above. You don't have to worry about that. She sure seems to get herself into predicaments, though, doesn't she?"

"Yes, she certainly does."

Ken sat down across from him. "We haven't come up with anything new to tell you about Natalie's murder. But I think there was something you were going to tell me that day when you stopped by my cottage and found Kate."

Clearing his throat, Spencer decided he might as well tell him. "There was a phone call to Scotland Yard, made by what sounded like a woman. The caller said that she knew who Natalie's killer was and that she was sure he was going to strike again. So that's why I contacted you."

"Who do you think it was?" Ken asked, rather doubting the Yard had any idea.

"Not sure. Still interviewing suspects. Could have been a man disguising his voice. Maybe even a crank call. We get our share of those."

164

Standing up, Ken said, "That's all I wanted to hear. I'll be on my way then."

"Goodbye. And now there are two damn cases to solve!" Spencer grumbled and turned back to the stack of folders on his desk.

CHAPTER 36

Later that evening Kate came down to dinner. She looked like herself again, fresh and lovely, wearing a pale green linen dress that set off her eyes.

Ken proudly showed Kate the medal she had earned. Kate took it in her hands and examined it like she had never seen a shiny object before. Then she held it to her heart and looked at Ken.

"I am so proud of you, Kate. Your efforts have been rewarded."

"Thank you, I will cherish this all my life. At least I've done something to make the world a better place."

"You certainly have."

As Kate sat down to dinner, she wondered what Robertson had told Ken and Fred. She didn't have to wonder long.

Fred spoke first. "So, we were filled in on your discussions with Mr. Robertson. My only question is, why did you agree to meet Dexter?"

So much for polite small talk, thought Kate. "I had received a note, which I thought was from him, asking me to come by at ten that morning. I thought perhaps he had information about Natalie's murder. Now I realize that it was a set-up and he didn't send the note."

There was a moment of silence and then Kate added, "It was not a romantic liaison, if that's what you're thinking."

"Of course, we don't think that," Ken spoke up as he casually took a bite of his dinner.

Fred did not comment.

"Obviously, someone else wrote that note and had intentions of killing Dexter and making me look responsible. Dexter did tell me he was writing an important expose." Kate was annoyed she had to defend herself. She had hoped Robertson would have allayed Fred's suspicions about her. The look she gave Fred conveyed her dismay.

Fred glanced away and turned his attention to the food on his plate.

"It's done, it's over," Ken said kindly. "We won't mention your visit to Dexter's house or your night in jail to anyone we know, that includes Anna and Travis. Isn't that right, Fred?"

"Of course, let's get on with our lives and never mention it again."

Kate spoke up, "If it's okay with you, I would like to let Anna know what happened. We have become friends and I don't think I can keep a secret from her."

"Yes, Anna is the epitome of discretion, you can trust her – I always have," Ken said. With a smile, he continued, "And we are now officially off the case. Robertson's orders."

"Yes, he told me that as well."

"He also said that most of your memory has come back."

Kate looked at Ken, trying to gauge his thoughts. She wasn't surprised that Robertson had told them about her memory coming back but she felt a little guilty about not being completely forthcoming with him and that he had to hear it from another source. Was this how Ken felt when he didn't tell her about her injury and why she was staying at his cottage and she had to hear about it from Detective Spencer?

"Yes," she acknowledged. "After talking to Robertson, who filled in a lot of the gaps, I now remember a lot of my past. It seems to be coming back in chronological order."

"Well, that's a good thing, right? With a memory, you can function and feel like yourself again. Maybe you'll remember friends and relatives soon," Ken sounded encouraging.

"Yes, that is a good thing. Although, there are things I would like to forget and probably can't remember because they are too terrible. They call it repressed memories." She continued, "Now, as to 'who I am' – that will always be an ongoing question, won't it? I spent over five years pretending to be someone I wasn't. I may never have the strong sense of self that some women have."

"That's a good point, some women are so full of themselves," Ken mused, "and you don't seem to be one of them. In any case, we would all like to forget some things and it's probably best if we do."

"I do remember how I met you in Germany," Kate said to Ken with a smile.

He looked at her for a moment, then looked down as he delicately cut the meat on his plate. He didn't respond.

After a few moments, Fred looked at Kate and she could see his opinion of her was starting to change. She had always thought that, although friendly and polite, he didn't think she was up to his standards for Ken and their family. Although, perhaps that didn't matter now since Fred was aware that she was not actually engaged to marry Ken.

"Kate," Fred said, "Our family is honored that you saved Ken's life while serving our country. We owe you a huge debt."

"Fred, I'm grateful I could do so. Anna told me about your service in the Great War and I applaud you for what you did."

The three continued their dinner in silence, each lost in their own thoughts. Kate retired to her room shortly after finishing, citing a headache she felt was coming on.

Lost Secrets

CHAPTER 37

A beautiful summer morning greeted them as they sat down to breakfast the next morning.

Earlier, Kate had a chance to explain everything to Anna. The words came tumbling out after Anna had knocked on her door to wake her up. To her surprise, Anna was not at all disappointed or concerned that Kate went to see Dexter and had never for one moment thought she was capable of murder. Kate realized that no matter what the future held, she had found a true friend.

"How is Miranda?" Kate asked.

"She is over the moon! She and Jeremy have been dating and I have never seen her so happy."

"That's great news, and how are you doing?"

"Fit as a fiddle, thanks for asking."

"Of course."

"Come downstairs, I have prepared a special breakfast. Ken is waiting for us."

****

"Thank you, Anna," Kate said as she placed her napkin on her lap and was served a perfectly cooked Eggs Benedict.

Anna nodded her head in a discreet reply, smiling slightly as she performed her typical housekeeping duties about the room, making sure the two of them had enough food on their plate and warm cups of tea.

Fred entered and joined the two at the table. Anna served his plate and tea.

Ken looked at Kate. "I've been thinking about this. After all you've been through, how about a nice evening out tonight?

You've had enough drama these last few days," he said as he sipped his tea, wondering how she would respond.

"That would be lovely, but I wouldn't want to impose."

"Nonsense," Ken said, "You could never be an imposition. Can you spare the Rolls tonight, Uncle Fred?"

"Yes, please take it."

"We may as well as ride in style."

"It is an impressive automobile," Kate said as she delicately sliced into her breakfast.

"That's settled, then. Excellent. Should we leave around six? Dinner and dancing, an evening to enjoy and one to remember."

"That sounds like heaven." Kate was thrilled, and spent the afternoon deciding what to wear and composing herself. She would be carefree for once and enjoy her evening with Ken.

Punctually at six, Ken knocked on Kate's room and she opened the door. Ken gasped at how lovely Kate looked in a light blue off-the-shoulder party dress with a sheer chiffon stole. Around her neck was a row of faux pearls that Ken had purchased for the evening. An elusive scent, like roses in the rain, filled his nostrils. He had not paid much notice to her appearance since they had been in London. His mind had been occupied with the wedding, business affairs and investigating the murder. This was the first time since their arrival they were going out to have fun together, no investigating or play acting – just a real and honest date – for the first time since they met.

"You look stunning in that dress," Ken said as he ushered her down the stairs.

"Thank you, Anna helped me pick out this dress today. And you, you're looking smart, that suit is perfection. Your tailor certainly has an eye for fashion."

Outside, Ken stood at the passenger side of the door and opened it for Kate as she got in, then closed the door behind her. He slid into the seat beside her and started the engine. The car glided forward, circled along the drive and cruised onto the main road.

Looking sideways at her, he spoke in a formal, almost cool tone. "I'm sorry you should have had such a bad few days."

"Yes, it was rather beastly." She looked at Ken but he was staring intently at the road.

"Anyway, I would rather not think about that tonight," she said as she looked down at her hands.

"Good plan. Let's focus on the future. More precisely, tonight, where would you like to go?"

With a broad smile, Kate responded, "You know London better than I, you pick the place."

With that said, Ken accelerated the Rolls, taking advantage of its power, and off they flew. A tram flashed past them, and all of a sudden they were in the heart of the restaurant and nightclub section of London. It seemed like they were weaving in and out of traffic, almost non-stop. Ken was a wonderful driver but took a few risks, Kate thought as she clutched her purse.

"How about Ritsons?"

"Ritsons?" asked Kate. "Isn't that a nightclub?" She had heard about the place, and that anyone with a standing turned up at Ritsons sooner or later."

"Yes, after a dinner at Brook's fine restaurant, let's go to Ritsons"

"Am I dressed all right?"

"You look lovely. Everyone's eyes will be on us when we walk in."

Dinner at Brook's was delicious and the wine was perfection. Kate gave her compliments to the chef and sommelier. Their conversation was lighthearted and pleasant. Then they were off to Ritsons.

After the host seated them at a small table against a back wall, they sipped cocktails. Down on the floor below, there was a whirlwind of music and dancing. Ken slipped off his dinner jacket and rose.

"Let's dance."

Kate knew she and Ken danced well together. They smoothly danced in unison, smiling at each other almost constantly. After four or five dances, foxtrots and jitter-bugs, the two were ready for a break. Still a bit out of breath from the activity, they headed towards their table. Ken didn't sit down though, because a few of his friends came by to give him their regards, and he stood chatting with them for a few moments before he had a chance to pull out his chair.

While Ken was occupied, Kate looked around the club and was surprised to see Amanda sitting toward the back of the club at a small table, surrounded by gentlemen. No doubt they were potential suitors. Was one of them her date? Kate was pleased to see she was out and about instead of moping at home. Not that she didn't have a good reason to do so, Kate thought.

"Should we go say hello to Amanda?" Kate suggested to Ken when he finally sat down to join her. At that moment, Amanda noticed them and waved a greeting from across the room.

"She looks rather occupied at the moment," Ken said as he waved back to Amanda. "It could be rather dangerous trying to cut in on her many admirers. She has had so many men wanting to spend time with her. I'm surprised she's still unmarried."

"Ken, I haven't seen you in ages," said a muscular young man, apparently another school chum of Ken's who stopped at their table. "And who is this lovely creature?"

"Kate, I would like you to meet Henry. We were at university together."

"It's a pleasure to meet you," Kate said standing and offering her hand.

"The pleasure is mine," Henry said as he took Kate's hand. After a little small talk and reminiscing, Henry left to mingle with other patrons and Ken and Kate sat back down at the table, alone at last.

"You certainly know a lot of people in town. Are you going to stay in London, buy a place here?" Kate asked. She wondered what Ken was thinking about for his own future. He no longer had to stay at the country cottage and worry about her. Kate knew he had a high social standing and obviously had a lot of friends here. She now had a better appreciation of the sacrifice he had made to stay with her in the country while she recovered from her injuries and waited to find out some of her history.

"Yes, I probably will." Ken's eyes were lost in the distance, he was looking down but appeared lost in thought.

After a few moments, he looked at her in a serious manner. "I know this was supposed to be just a light-hearted night out," he remarked as he sipped his whisky cocktail. "But I should tell you about some recent developments in the case."

"Please tell me, what has happened?" Kate asked, surprised at this revelation.

"George Cresswell is under investigation for Dexter's murder. In 1939, he was a member of a group that tried to negotiate peace with Germany without knowledge or approval of the government, he could be arrested."

Kate recalled that Dexter had told her about this. "What is George saying about this? Have you talked to him?"

"He told me that he was a member of such a group at one time but disassociated himself from them long before they took any illegal actions. Since then he has done everything possible to help the war effort. As you know, his son, Andrew even volunteered for service."

"Why would George's activities be of concern now? George only had a brief association with this group."

"George was in the area where Dexter lived on the day he was killed so they think there may be a connection. They never were on friendly terms since Dexter exposed the group back then."

"George was in the area?"

"Yes, I saw him there myself."

"What? You were in Dexter's neighborhood the day he was killed?"

"Yes, I went to the tailor to have this jacket altered. His shop is on the same street."

"Who is making these allegations about George?"

"Edward."

"The Member of Parliament?"

"Yes, you have met him before, several times."

"Yes, I know who he is but…." Kate didn't finish her sentence as she started thinking about how many people's lives had been turned upside down by suspicions that were never proved, with no chance to defend themselves.

Ken took the last swallow from his drink and put down the glass. "I've had enough. Let's go for a drive," he said, interrupting her thoughts.

They left Ritsons together, holding hands. The car awaited them in a small by-street, narrow and dark. Ken held the door open for her, always the gentleman. It was hard for Kate to let go of his hand and step inside. Holding his hand felt so right. She smiled as she settled in and he closed the door.

Apparently their night wasn't quite over. Ken drove Kate to a private club with an unmarked front door.

"Darling, I don't know your feelings about this, but now and then I do like to do a bit of gambling," he said, watching her eyes carefully. "Do you fancy games of chance?"

"Let's go," she responded, ready to try anything, as long as she was with Ken.

After Ken knocked on the door in a certain sequence, a black-gloved rather large gentleman opened the door and, after looking them over, escorted them to an open table near the back of the darkly-lit room.

Drinks were ordered and immediately served by attractive and scantily dressed young women. Several other men and women showed up at their table and Ken and Kate were dealt into a round of cards. Luck was with Kate and after she won several hands, she cleaned up the table. She laughed at her good fortune and they both agreed they should leave while she was ahead of the game. Ken didn't know about the endless nights she'd had to spend playing poker with several of her German companions to pass the time when she was stationed in Germany.

The drive back to Sir Fred's house felt like it was too quick. Ken parked the car and faced her.

"Did you have a good time? Be honest with me."

"Yes, it was heavenly."

At that response, he surprised her and moved closer to her. For a brief moment, he held his arms around her, his face brushed up against hers and Kate thought he would kiss her. There was a flash between them that felt wonderful. Then he turned away, quickly jumped out of the car and opened her door, extending his hand to take hers. They silently walked into the house, still holding hands. Ken saw her to her door, the two said their respective goodnights, both not sure how to handle what just happened.

Ken turned and walked toward his room. As Kate closed the door behind her, she leaned her back against the door. She realized she was in love with Ken Michaels. Love was one of those repressed memories, repressed feelings that now she was fully aware of.

CHAPTER 38

The next morning Kate came downstairs to find Ken sitting at the table, apparently waiting for her. He was reading the newspaper. He had finished his breakfast and his teacup was empty.

"Ah, there you are." His eyes were welcoming. He folded the paper and placed it on the adjacent bureau. "Any thoughts on what you'd like to do today, now that you're back with the living? You seemed to enjoy yourself last night."

"I did indeed and I am feeling better. It was a lovely diversion, thank you so very much." She smiled back at him. "I'm thinking I should start looking for my own flat."

"You don't have to do that, Kate. Fred is happy to have you stay here. And I'd like you to stay here too, for as long as you'd like."

"I can put that off for a while, I suppose," she responded. Maybe there was hope for the two of them. She was reluctant to ask about the status of their relationship. Best to keep it impersonal and casual. She wouldn't want to scare him off by seeming to make demands of him. It was nice that he cared and made the offer.

Kate also wondered how serious Ken had been regarding them giving up their research into the two murders. "So, what do you think of our acquiescing to the powers that be and holding off on our own investigation?"

"I'm having second thoughts. How about you?"

"I'm with you all the way. Any ideas about what to look for next?"

"Not really. I won't have much time spend on that effort, though. I have to attend to some business that I've been neglecting. There are a lot of post-war opportunities. I can no longer slack off my responsibilities since a lot of people are counting on me."

"I understand."

"Besides, I don't want to put you in danger anymore."

Kate shuddered. She remembered how Robertson had said she might be in danger herself. She didn't want Ken to worry about her. "It's cool in this room," she said instead of expressing her worrisome thoughts. The rain had started first thing in the morning and it was looking to be a cold and dreary day.

"It's cool in Scotland, too, at this time of year," Ken said, changing the subject to one close to his heart. "I have the pleasure of inviting you to our annual hiking and fishing excursion that's going on this weekend. One last relaxing holiday before I buckle down to business. All of the usual social crowd meet up at a lodge near Aviemore, in the Scottish Highlands. The accommodations are spacious, elegant, and there is a large meeting room that is very comfortable with a huge fireplace. The mountains are incredible. You don't have to hike or fish if you don't want to, lots of people just sit by the fire and talk or read. Are you interested?"

"I am! Sounds wonderful! I would love to hike and fish, it sounds like a true adventure. And I don't recall ever traveling in Scotland, I imagine it is lovely there."

"I'm glad to hear you say that," Ken said, relieved. He'd been concerned she would bow out of events associated with his circle of friends. "Trust me, you won't believe your eyes. The scenery is breath-taking. After all we've been through recently, I think this is what we truly need – an adventure and a jolly good time. Fresh air, blue skies, the wholesomeness of nature. What could go wrong?"

"Right you are," Kate agreed, although she wondered if it was such a good idea for her to go. They would have to keep up their relationship façade. And most certainly one of their social group was likely to be a murderer. But worrying about it wouldn't help.

Another consideration entered Kate's mind. "I don't have any clothes to wear that would be appropriate for that type of outing."

"No worries, Kate. Use my charge account at Harrod's as you have been doing and buy whatever you need for the weekend."

"I sincerely appreciate your help until I get back on my feet. Now as far as my plans for today, I'd like to go through Natalie's room again, and spend some time with Amanda whom I have been meaning to call."

"Suit yourself, I'm going to attend to some last minute details about a deal I'm working on."

Ken was pleased she was making friends and becoming close to the cousin of whom he was very fond. "After a few hours of business, I'll go to the club then and play tennis with Andrew. Looks like their indoor court today, due to the rain."

"How is he taking the investigation of his dad?"

"Not well, as you can imagine. His family have made sacrifices for our country and the war effort. He doesn't understand why anyone would be making accusations to the contrary."

"Well, I'm sure it will all be cleared up soon. It must be hard on both Andrew and George, not to mention Elaine, having that pressure put on them."

"Yes, indeed. And I'm afraid George is not very happy with me. I got him involved in a business venture that did not pay off, I'm afraid he lost some money."

"Well, I'm sure you had the best of intentions."

"Yes, I lost money in the venture as well. At least now I have investments that are more of a sure thing and I'll pass this information along to George. Hopefully, I can win over his trust again."

Kate was glad to have an explanation of why George seemed to give Ken the cold shoulder when they first met. Business can turn friends into enemies, she mused.

Ken stood up and looked at her. "Are you sure you'll be okay today? Fred won't be home either."

"Yes, I'm fine. Have a good time playing tennis. I'm going to just relax this afternoon."

"Alright, I'm off then. See you later."

At least he was keeping her in the loop and being friendly. As soon as Ken was out the door, Kate grabbed the newspaper that he had been reading. She had been wondering what was in the paper about Dexter's murder. She saw that the paper from the day earlier was there on the bureau as well. That one had an article on the front page 'London Journalist Murdered: Police are investigating'. She hesitated to read on but had to see what everyone had read about the murder. The article named Dexter Flynn as the victim and stated a German national as the person under suspicion, to her chagrin. It read that the suspect was found at the scene of the murder and she was being held for questioning. Would anyone in Ken's circle suspect it might have been her? Thank God she was only in jail overnight and released the next day.

On the current day's paper, the headlines were on to something else, to Kate's surprise and relief. She wondered if Robertson had something to do with the paper's decision to refrain from printing further stories about the murder or to print her name. She knew the investigation would be top secret and they would only throw out tidbits to the press, at least until the murder was solved.

Placing the papers back where she found them, she picked up the phone on the bureau and called the number Amanda had given her days before.

A housekeeper answered and said she would bring Amanda to the phone.

"Hello, this is Amanda," said a weary voice.

"Amanda, this is Kate. Would you like to meet for lunch today?"

"Why, yes, I would like that," Amanda said, sounding a bit more cheerful. "How about that quaint French café down the street from your house, I mean Fred's house, on the north side of the street. At noon?

"Perfect. See you there. Goodbye."

As Kate put down the phone she wondered if stories of the murder had reached Amanda, but perhaps not. Amanda knew Dexter and probably would have mentioned it. And she seemed to keep herself above rumors and speculation and seemed to have a sharp mind without a personal agenda. That was probably one of the reasons she enjoyed Amanda's company.

CHAPTER 39

The café was crowded. Kate saw Amanda in a far corner and quickly crossed the room to join her. The waitress appeared before they had a chance to talk, and they both ordered tea, croissants, small salads and sandwiches. After the waitress left, Kate started the conversation.

"Amanda, you sounded so sad when I called," Kate said with concern in her voice. "What's going on?"

"I ran into Raj yesterday at the market. I didn't want a confrontation but he came up to me." She continued to tell Kate that Raj indicated he still had strong feelings for her, and that's why he hasn't married the woman he had been promised to, despite the concerns and pressure from his family. Raj also confided in Amanda that the woman herself had backed out of the agreement just a few days ago. Apparently, she and her parents were tired of waiting. His parents were very distraught at the cancellation of a wedding they had planned for years, but Raj told Amanda that he was deeply relieved.

The waitress arrived with their tea. She also brought croissants and sandwiches on a tray and placed their small salads in front of them. The two thanked the server and both started eating, with Kate listening while Amanda continued her story.

"Raj also asked if I would allow him to call on me and take me out. This was against his parents' wishes, but it was something he said he wanted to do.

Kate was very surprised by this new development. "And how do you feel about this?" she inquired.

"I will admit I still hold deep feelings for Raj. How could I not? He was the father of my child. I have felt strongly for him from the time we met, and I try to have no regrets about what happened.

It's not healthy to hold onto negative feelings, although I admit sometimes I break down and cry about it. A good cry seems to be the best therapy for a broken heart."

"You have certainly been through a lot," Kate said soothingly. "Life is always throwing us curves, especially when we aren't expecting it."

"At this point, as you can well imagine, I am uncertain what to do. I'm afraid that his parents will find some way to sabotage our relationship if we began to see each other again. They will never let us be together, of that I'm sure."

"What did you tell Raj?"

"Before I could answer, his demeanor became very serious and sad, he had tears in his eyes and looked like he was going to tell me something else. He choked up and could barely speak. That's when I told him to stop, that I could not listen to anything more he had to say, and I ran out of the market, leaving my groceries behind."

"Maybe it wasn't an accident that you ran into him in the market, perhaps he staked out and watched for you. When he saw you, he followed you because he wanted to talk to you in a public setting. He probably knew you wouldn't see him at your home."

"That's possible." Amanda conceded, "He does know that I go to that market frequently."

"Amanda, you are the sweetest person I've ever met. Ken and I will support you in whatever you decide. If you still have any feelings for Raj, I hope you will act upon them. To find someone you truly love is rare."

"You sound like you speak from experience."

Kate did not respond. She hoped with all her heart that things would work out for Amanda. She had been through so much and deserved better.

The waitress interrupted them, asking, "Would you like some dessert?" She showed them a tray of sample delights. Both ordered a small piece of pound cake.

It seemed like it was Kate's turn to talk. She asked Amanda what she had heard about Dexter's murder and found out she hadn't been aware of it. Amanda was saddened and expressed her shock at hearing of a seemingly senseless and brutal murder but confided that she did not know Dexter well. Kate did not give the details of her involvement in any of it. Amanda was dealing with enough drama for one week.

"Will the killing ever end?" Amanda commented as she took a bite of her tart.

The two chatted about less worrisome topics and found they had a lot in common in many ways. Time was flying by and they had several cups of tea after finishing their lunch.

"Kate, what about you and Ken? Have you set a date?"

"We haven't yet," Kate said, relieved that Amanda didn't suspect anything about the charade they'd been putting on and hoping she could keep up the ruse with what was becoming a close friendship. Lord, she hated deceiving friends. "Amanda, I'll let you know, don't worry, you'll be first on my list to know anything. You can help pick out my dress and help with the arrangements."

Amanda smiled and sipped her tea. "That would be lovely! I'll look forward to it. What about your family? When will we meet them? Won't your mum want to be involved in helping you pick out your dress?'

Unprepared for the question, Kate stammered and answered that her parents had passed on and that she was an only child.

Please don't press for details.

"Oh, I'm sorry to hear about your parents."

"Thank you. I would rather not talk about it now, it's a long story and I prefer to keep my grief private."

"I understand." Then after a brief pause, she said, "You have really captured our Ken's heart. He told me that you saved his life twice."

"Twice?" Kate was taken aback and could not hide the surprise on her face. "Did he say what he meant by that?"

"No. I have no idea but I'm sure you know," Amanda said with a twinkle in her eyes.

"I really have no idea," Kate replied trying to assume a casual and pleasant demeanor.

"He must have meant that your love has given him new life. I think he's been pretty lonely and waiting for the right woman to come along."

"What about Jolene? I somehow feel that I'm barging in on a relationship that has been brewing for a while. You should see the way she looks at me. And looks at him."

Amanda laughed, "Jolene? Good God, I doubt it, although I know she has been after him for some time. She was a friend of Natalie and in their circle. I don't believe he has ever returned her affections. Jolene has a domineering personality and needs someone she can dominate. That certainly would not be Ken. Jolene and Andrew were in love once and I think they will be an item again, if they aren't already. I saw them together at Ritsons one night last week. Andrew is a talented and intelligent young man with a bright future, he is not a lost cause just because he is having trouble adjusting back to civilian life. He'll be fine."

"Thank you, that means a lot to me. Ken is a very special man but I wouldn't want to interfere if they were involved. Or if they had a romantic relationship before I met him."

"He is indeed, a very special and caring man. Kate, don't worry, you aren't coming between them. You will feel more comfortable with his friends and relations once you get to know us and spend more time with us. Again, I'll ask, we haven't scared you off, have we?"

"No, everyone has been very kind."

"Well, I hope they have been on their best behavior."

A few moments of silence passed while they drank their tea.

Kate then asked what was on her mind. "You don't believe in lost causes, do you? Is that why, you and Raj, is that why you haven't found a partner? Ken said you have many eligible suitors.

He and I would have had to fight our way through a crowd of adoring men just to talk to you at the nightclub last night."

Amanda smiled and laughed at the suggestion but then the smile left Amanda's face. She looked serious but said nothing.

"I don't wish to upset you, it is none of my business. Please forget I mentioned it."

"No, that's alright, it's a perfectly reasonable question."

Seeking a different topic, she asked Amanda, "Are you coming to the Scottish get-together?"

"No, I'm not. It is tempting and should be great fun, but I want to be alone this weekend and do some soul-searching. I'm not up for a lot of social interaction. Anyway, the Patels will be there and I have no desire to see them. At some point I have to make peace with them but I'm not there yet."

The real reason, Kate thought.

Amanda continued, "Are you and Ken going?"

"Yes, I'm excited at the prospect of a fun get-away."

"I'm sure you will have a wonderful time. It is a charming area and the accommodations are delightful."

"Thank you. I have never been to Scotland and am looking forward to the trip."

It seemed like a good time to end their luncheon. Kate paid the bill, they said their goodbyes and agreed to meet again soon. Kate glanced at her watch and realized it was already half past two.

CHAPTER 40

Back at Fred's house, Kate got down to the business of finding anything the police may have missed when they first investigated the murder. She walked immediately to Natalie's rooms. Neither Fred nor Ken were home and it looked like Anna was out as well. Natalie's rooms had not changed since the day she died. The desk in her office contained only a typewriter. There were no papers near it or on the desk. Kate got on her knees and looked in the filing drawers in the desk. She found lots of articles Natalie had written, first drafts, ideas she had drafted for potential articles. They were in disarray from when the police had gone through the drawers. Kate realized that the room had been fully searched during the investigation. Nothing jumped out at her as being important.

Kate then went into Natalie's bedroom and perused her closet. She found a pretty light-weight raincoat and, on impulse, tried it on. There was a mirror on the other side of the room and Kate looked at herself in the mirror to see how the coat fit. Imitating models she had seen in magazines, she put her hands inside the pockets and turned to see the side view of herself in the mirror with the coat on. Then she found something odd. Inside the right-hand pocket she could feel an envelope. Most likely, the police would have noticed the coat but might not have carefully checked all of the pockets. No-one would have found the envelope unless they were very patient and observant, or specifically looking for it. Pulling it out, she noticed it appeared to have been sealed at one time but looked like it had been opened and lightly re-sealed. There was no postmark so it must have been hand delivered.

Kate conjectured that perhaps Natalie found it on the doorstep when she had come home. She took the coat off, hung it back up, walked over to the desk, sat down and opened the envelope. Inside it was a short hand-written note. She could see that it was from Dexter because it was on his personalized stationery. It read:

"Natalie Dearest, please don't be coy with me. I know that you know something. Do you value your life? I know your uncle is out of town, so we can talk privately. I'll be around this evening. Please, Natalie, don't be foolish."

Kate was baffled and astonished. Her mind tried to process what she had just read. Natalie was strangled. She checked the date on the letter and realized it was the day that Natalie died.

What did this letter mean? Should she show this to Ken? Who had read this note and resealed the envelope? Was it Natalie or someone else? Ken had been in this room many times before. This note implicated Dexter, the man she thought she knew and thought she might have had a future with. Apparently she never knew him much at all. Could Dexter have killed Natalie because she found out something about him, was he involved in something nefarious? The police said that all the papers on Natalie's desk had been taken away. If Dexter had done it, he would not have any idea his letter was in her coat pocket. He may had searched for it and couldn't find it.

Then dark thoughts ran through her mind and her blood ran cold. Ken. Dexter murdered. Could Ken have found and read the note and surmised that Dexter was the killer? Ken had told her in no uncertain terms that he would avenge his sister's murder. They had discussed that Dexter may have gotten in the way of Natalie and Andrew's relationship as they spent a lot of time together. And Ken clearly didn't seem to like Dexter. Were these motives for homicide? The gun used to shoot Dexter was military issue, like several that Ken owned. By his own admission, he was in the neighborhood the day that Dexter was shot. He said he was there to have his jacket altered but she knew that his tailor did not have his shop in that area. She had gone with him once to the tailor for alterations on one of her dresses and it was in a different location.

But surely Ken would not want to frame her. He didn't even know that she was going there that morning, she hadn't told him. She had been assuming that the person who wrote the note asking her to see Dexter that fateful day was the person that killed him, but maybe not. Perhaps Dexter himself wrote the note. Sometimes things don't always happen the way that they appear.

Was it coincidence that she arrived after Dexter was shot? Maybe a neighbor called the police when they heard the shot. Deep in thought, she hadn't heard that someone had entered the room.

"Hi Kate, find something interesting?"

Kate jumped as she looked up and saw Ken standing behind her, just a few feet away. With shaky hands, she put the letter back in the envelope, trying to act as if everything was fine, and then put both discretely inside the top drawer of the desk.

"I was just hoping to find some evidence that the police may have missed. I haven't found anything of interest." She forced a smile. "How was your game?" she asked as she stood up, facing Ken with her back against the desk.

"It was grand. Andrew was a tough competitor. He has been working on his serve and I'd say he is ready to move to the next level of play at our club."

"I'm sure he will excel with practice since he loves the game. You are a great friend to help him reach his full potential."

"Well, I love it too. If I remember right, you enjoy the game yourself. We will have to play doubles with him and Amanda. Would you like that?"

"Yes, I would enjoy that."

"We'll arrange for it then."

"I'll look forward to it."

"Is anything wrong? You look a little pale."

"No, everything's fine."

"How was your lunch with Amanda?"

"It was delightful, we went to that new French café."

"Splendid. By the way, I will be leaving town on business tomorrow early in the morning and I'll be gone until late afternoon, but how about dinner tomorrow night? I have Italian in mind."

Kate stared at Ken wondering if her new suspicions could possibly be true. He did not ask about the letter that she had in her hand when he came in or seem to acknowledge it.

"What's the matter, don't you like Italian?"

She broke out of her thoughts and said, "Yes, of course, I love Italian food."

Ken was concerned. Kate agreed to dinner but without the enthusiasm he was expecting. And it seemed like she was hiding something. He didn't always understand women and hoped it wasn't something he'd said that had upset her. He chose to ignore how stilted and different she was acting.

"Great, I'll make reservations. Say about seven?"

"Yes, seven is fine. I'll look forward to it."

CHAPTER 41

The next morning, after Ken left, Kate returned to Natalie's office and put the letter she had found back where it had been, in Natalie's coat pocket. She looked through a few more papers in the desk, studying everything until she felt like she practically knew Natalie. Not finding anything of interest, she asked Travis to take her back to the library.

Heading back to the room Dexter had showed her in the library, she went through as many articles as she could find that were within the timeframe of the months and days leading up to Natalie's murder. Articles Natalie had written and editorials that Dexter had written did not reveal anything out of the ordinary. From her research, and based on her gut feeling, she was certain that Dexter did not kill Natalie. However, she was not certain whether or not Ken thought he did, if he had read the letter. Ken did not know Dexter well and that letter seemed to incriminate him.

Remembering the last time she was at the library, she thought about Dexter, who had so much potential and could be such a kind and dedicated man. If dead men could tell tales......

Kate asked the receptionist if there was a phone she could use. Sitting at an unoccupied desk, she phoned Mr. Robertson to go over again exactly what Dexter had said to him when they met at the library. The conversation did not answer any of Kate's questions. George Cresswell had been cleared of any further suspicion and Robertson did not have any more leads in the investigation of Dexter's murder.

Kate took a taxi home, as she had asked Travis not to wait for her. During the ride, she pondered what Ken might have done. Another thing that caused her concern was that after Dexter's murder, Ken seemed less interested in pursuing the investigation into Natalie's murder. Did he feel that he had not only solved that mystery but exacted his revenge? It was painful to be thinking this but, in her experience not everyone was whom they appeared to be. Should she confront him or forget about it? She finally decided let to sleeping dogs lie, as they say.

Later that afternoon, Ken arrived back at the house from his business trip. Kate and Anna were out working in the garden. Anna had been trimming the rosebush and Kate decided to go out and help her. It was good to be outside and the roses smelled wonderful. Anna stopped her work as soon as she saw Ken and doted on him as usual. Kate kept clipping, and Ken was somewhat disappointed in the chilly reception he received from her. Although she smiled and waved at him, he knew her well enough to realize something was on her mind. He went to his study to finish some paperwork, somewhat perturbed.

Kate walked to her room, wondering how she was going to act as if everything was fine. She prepared for her date with Ken, picking out from the wardrobe an emerald green satin dress which Ken had bought for her. The dress had a wide boat-neck collar and was fitted perfectly. It was the dress that was altered by Ken's tailor. Wearing it might make him realize that she knew exactly where his tailor was located. She put on the string of faux pearls and wore white gloves with a clutch purse. Closing her door, she sighed deeply and put a smile on her face.

"Ready?" he inquired as Kate came down the stairs He was dressed in a dark suit tailored and looked smart. "You look lovely, my dear."

"Thank you, and yes, I'm ready and I'm hungry as well."

"You'll love this place. I have never been there, but my friends say it's one of the best in town."

The restaurant was full of Italian charm, dimly lit tables with candles, pictures of Venetian gondolas on the walls, red and white checked tablecloths. They were seated in a corner where there was privacy. The waiter was attentive, bringing a bottle of fine Barolo, and the dinner was delicious and well-served. They were treated to spumoni ice cream for dessert. Kate acted like her cheerful self and the conversation centered on the upcoming trip to Scotland. She realized that this get-away was exactly what she needed to clear her head. Perhaps a new setting would help her process the many scenarios that could prove to solve the two murders. However, the more she thought about it, the more she suspected Ken and her hopes and dreams were fading in a state of dazed confusion.

They drove home and Ken walked Kate up to her room. As he said goodnight, he leaned in to kiss her goodnight. This was the kiss that Kate had wanted, dreamt about for years. As her memory came back, she recalled how smitten she was when she first met him in Germany. He was a most attractive and charming man. However, her new suspicions had a grip on her and at that moment she remembered Dexter's bloody body, lying on his living room floor. Ken looked surprised as she quickly turned her cheek away and opened her door, saying a quiet and subdued good night without looked back at him.

Ken stopped her from closing the door in his face. Looking at her questioningly, he said quietly, "Kate, what is going on? I thought you were starting to have feelings for me. I must have misread the signals. I'm sorry if that's the case. Women are very hard to understand, but I'm trying."

He looked very sincere, but Kate was overwhelmed with mixed emotions.

"Is that it? Are you not interested in me – in that way?" he asked.

Not being able to keep her suspicions to herself any longer, looking at Ken straight in the eyes, she blurted out, "It's…..the letter. I found the letter."

"What letter?"

"The letter I was reading in Natalie's room, yesterday afternoon when you came in the door. It was in her coat pocket, unopened, but I could tell it had been opened before. I know you saw it. I think you read it and know exactly what I'm referring to."

"I honestly have no idea what you are talking about."

She stared at him, suspicion clouding her lovely green eyes.

"Please enlighten me," he said with a quizzical look on his face.

"You said you were in Dexter's neighborhood when he was shot. I don't remember you saying that you were going to see your tailor that day and I know that your tailor is on the other side of town. The gun that killed Dexter was military issue – like guns you own and have access to."

"If you must know, my regular tailor was in France on holiday and I went instead to another shop that a friend recommended that day." Then there was a silence as Ken processed what Kate saying and realized what she was suggesting.

"Good God, are you accusing me of murdering Dexter?"

"I opened the letter," said a voice from down the hall.

Ken and Kate both looked down the hall at Fred, as he approached them as they stood in front of Kate's room.

"That's right, I found the letter and opened it. I always believed Dexter killed Natalie and that letter confirmed my suspicions."

"What? Dexter killed Natalie, my dear sweet sister!" Ken exclaimed with astonishment.

"It was my suspicion," Fred said as casually as if he were talking about the weather. "Dexter and Natalie had a complicated relationship. Either they were arguing or they seemed to have some deep attraction to each other. I could never figure out if it was personal or professional." He looked directly at Kate. "He seemed to have an extraordinary effect on women, as you should know, my dear."

Kate blushed.

Fred continued, "I don't know how he felt when Natalie became engaged but I don't think he took it well and I know that bothered her. I always assumed he fancied her."

"Why didn't you say something?" Ken exclaimed, bewildered at what he was hearing and trying to comprehend it. "And what on earth is in this bloody letter?"

Kate spoke softly, "It's a cryptic letter from Dexter to Natalie that seems to threaten her."

Fred included both of them in his response. "I found the letter the day after Dexter was murdered. Why say something then? He was gone and wouldn't be able to answer the questions I had regarding the meaning of the letter or to defend himself. I didn't like him, but everyone deserves their day in court. If I had read the letter before that day, I would have asked him about it or taken it to the authorities."

"But how did you find it?" Kate asked.

"I found it when I was going through Natalie's clothes, as I was thinking about finally donating them to charity. The detectives must have missed it. It was sealed when I found it. I tried to reseal it but apparently our Miss Kate doesn't miss much."

"So, Natalie never opened the letter," Kate surmised.

"I assume not."

"No one opened the letter before you did, before Dexter was murdered."

"That is correct."

Kate looked at Fred, then looked at Ken, turning pink with embarrassment. All her conjectures were thrown out the window and she had as much as accused Ken of capital murder. All she could say was, "I see."

Ken demanded to see the letter for himself immediately, and Kate told them she had put it back in the coat pocket. Turning away, she walked into her room and closed the door. The two men went downstairs to find and read the letter.

Kate sat on her bed and put her face in her hands.

My God, what have I done? I have no future with Ken whatsoever now. I'll be lucky if he wants me as a friend. They will probably chuck me out of this house tomorrow, if not tonight. They must realize that I thought, although only for a short while, that Ken murdered Dexter after reading the letter. All because of my over-active imagination.

And now I will never get that kiss that I squandered away.

Lost Secrets

She had herself one of those good cries that Amanda had talked about.

CHAPTER 42

The next morning, to Kate's pleasant surprise, there was no eviction notice put underneath her door. Indeed, Ken and Fred acted like the events of the night before did not happen at all when Kate came down for breakfast. Neither one mentioned Kate leaving, in fact, Ken reminded her they were going on the Scotland trip in two days.

It looked like the murder of Natalie had been solved. Surely, Dexter killed Natalie, whether it was because of rejection of his romantic advances or some nefarious actions that Dexter was up to and Natalie found out about. Obviously, the letter that was found convicted Dexter of Natalie's murder in the minds of Fred and Ken. Both of them did not like Dexter, so he was a convenient person for them to blame. Kate had a different perspective based on her short relationship with him. No one would ever know the truth but they all decided there was no reason to continue any investigation.

After a brief discussion, all agreed that Ken would take the letter to Detective Spencer and let Scotland Yard come to their own conclusions. Surely it would be clear to them that Dexter murdered Natalie.

Ken and Kate did not talk much the next two days except for small talk during meals. Ken spent hours with his business dealings and was not home much of the day or evenings, trying to wrap up business loose ends before the trip. Kate had time to look at the books in Fred's library and found a few interesting ones, passing the afternoon time reading. She tried to forgive herself for her mistake since it looked like Ken had. She had a suspicious mind, and that was not surprising given her work in Germany, where she always had to anticipate possible occurrences. Ken did not kill Dexter. But someone else did. And she was certain his murder was not solved in any way.

Anticipating a pleasant trip to Scotland, she slept like a baby, dreaming about a beautiful forest with a young deer who would eat right out of your hand. What natural beauty and serenity would she be viewing on the weekend retreat?

The next afternoon Kate asked Anna if she was interested in going to Harrod's with her, and Travis brought them both to the store. Anna was kind and cheerful and followed Kate up and down the many floors to find appropriate fishing and hiking gear and clothes for her to wear. Anna was the picture of good manners and did not mention anything to Kate about the rift she could sense between her and Ken. Anna knew that every relationship had its ups and downs, and that most times they were worked through. These two young ones were well-matched, she thought, and surely be enjoying each other's company again soon.

CHAPTER 43

The weekend arrived and there was a hustle and bustle as the car was loaded and Fred, Ken and Kate settled into the back seat. Travis drove the Rolls to the train station and the three of them boarded the train to Aviemore. Waving goodbye to Travis from the window, they settled into their compartment for the ride. Everyone in the group of friends were to meet at the Inn for an evening meal at five.

Kate was rather subdued during the ride, looking out the window or at her hands. She was a bit nervous. Her intuition told her that in spite of the location, anything could happen with two unresolved mysterious murders. Her initial excitement about having never been to the Scottish Highlands now seemed secondary since she still had a lot weighing on her mind. She remembered who she would be at the Inn with.

Why did Ken invite her to this gathering? Now that he and Fred were satisfied as to the conclusion of the Natalie investigation, this would be a perfect time for Ken to say he broke off the engagement with Kate and send her on her way. Kate was perplexed why Ken would want to continue the charade of her acting as his fiancée.

Then there was another burden to carry. What if the authorities couldn't figure out who Dexter's killer was, and decided to look at her again, despite Robertson's objections? They might think she would be easy to convict, manufacture a motive, and then they would be credited for solving another murder. Time was ticking by – she had better find out who killed Dexter. There were so many unresolved questions about these two cases but Kate was sure they were connected. She didn't like the uncertainty but was well-trained on keeping her composure in tough times. This was one of those times.

She laughed at Ken's jokes, was pleased that he placed his arm around her now and then, but never met her eyes. Surely, he had some resentment from her outlandish accusation. Jolene might not be the perfect person for Ken but, chances are, she never accused Ken of murder. Kate vowed to make sure her imagination didn't get the best of her in the future.

These thoughts brought her mind back over the letter she found in Natalie's room. She pretended to Ken and Fred that the mystery was solved but she wasn't quite sure. There was another angle to this scenario. Maybe Dexter was not threatening Natalie but merely stating that Natalie was keeping information from him that he feared was very dangerous. If that was true, why would Natalie keep information from him? Was she about to let him in on her secret? Did Dexter show up at the house that night and find there was no answer – because Natalie had already been murdered?

At the Inn, she found out that Ken had reserved a two-bedroom side-by-side suite for the two of them, still keeping up appearances. Kate smiled when she was shown to her room by the bell-boy. The room was exquisitely decorated, fit for a princess. It was amazing to her that she could be staying at such a place. She was certain her adventures in the upper class were temporary at best. Soon she'd be back in London, looking for a job, probably scrimping to get by. It was nice of Ken to buy her a new suitcase so she'd still be looking the part. Such a dreamy man, she felt fortunate for the kindness he'd shown her and the chance to be in his life, even if it was for a short while.

She took a long time hanging up her clothes, settling into the room. She wanted to make an appearance after most of the guests had already had a drink or two, so as not to be the center of attention when she arrived. As soon as she headed down the main staircase to the large dining room, she heard laughter and clinking glasses. Her plan had worked; it appeared that she had entered the room unnoticed. A uniformed server appeared with a tray of drinks and hors-d'oeuvres. She picked up one of the glasses on the tray and a small cake, nodded and whispered a thank you to the server. An excellent champagne cocktail, it tasted wonderful, as did the cake.

Scanning the room, she noticed that no-one was seated. She saw Ken standing in a group of four, which included Andrew and Jolene. Continuing to look around the room, she wondered where exactly she should start mingling. She saw Mrs. Patel was there, as well as the usual crowd she had seen at the many parties she and Ken had attended.

Making small-talk with people she had briefly met before, she began to feel out of place. Ken hadn't even noticed her. She was wondering what had been said about her regarding Dexter and the fact that Ken was lavishing his attentions on Jolene when supposedly he was engaged to her. She finished her cocktail and placed the glass on a table as she walked out of the room.

Noticing there was a cigar bar area across the hall, she sat at a table and ordered a whisky and water on the rocks to calm her nerves a bit. Seated at the next table were Mr. Patel and another gentleman drinking whisky and smoking cigars. Kate held up her glass in acknowledgement of the two gentlemen. They in turn did the same. She noticed that they had been speaking together in English when she walked to her table but switched to French when she sat down, obviously to keep their conversation private. She was amused. They would never assume that she was fluent in French. She figured Mr. Patel already had her pegged for an uneducated lower-class secretary that somehow managed to win Ken's affections by some unseemly means. That was probably what most of the guests in the adjoining room thought. Kate sipped her drink and overheard the entire conversation.

She was shocked to hear what the two men were saying. Could it be true? It was hard to sit at the table and pretend she was not understanding what they were talking about, not to gasp or to confront the two men at the next table. Reminiscent of her time as a spy in Germany, she had to act unaffected, no change in color, no change in demeanor. One thing she knew for certain was that she had to contact Amanda as soon as possible. Should she try to call her now from Scotland? No, this was the kind of information you tell someone in person, not over the phone. They would be returning to London on Tuesday and Kate resolved to see Amanda first thing upon her return. Should she tell Ken what she had heard? No, not before she told Amanda, that wouldn't be right.

A white-coated man came in to announce that dinner was being served, and Mr. Patel and the other gentleman rose and walked in the direction of the dining room. Kate was behind them but Mr. Patel noticed her and graciously stepped behind her saying "After you, miss" as they entered the dining room.

"Thank you," Kate said with a sweet innocent smile that would not reveal that she knew exactly what had been said in the bar. She saw Ken and walked toward him, assuming they would be seated together at the table. Before she reached him, however, she was approached by Edward.

"Ah, it's nice to see you here," he said. They were standing at the side of the door, somewhat hidden from view from the main dining area. Taking her hand and kissing it, he continued, "You really are a most attractive woman. How did Ken manage to find you and sweep you off your feet?"

"Thank you very much," she replied, quite amused. *Is he flirting with me?* "You are too kind or perhaps you've had too much of the fine whisky they serve here."

Edward smiled and said, "I hope Ken doesn't have all of your time scheduled already, as I'd like you to join me and several others on a hike tomorrow morning. Have you been to the highlands before?"

"No, never."

"Well then, you must allow me to show you around."

"I'll check my social calendar and get back with you," she responded with a charming smile and turned away from him, heading toward the seat next to Ken.

"Let me know tonight," he said loudly to her as she turned to walk away.

The encounter was a bit startling to her as Edward had never shown interest or kindness toward her. Perhaps he had noticed she was feeling a bit out of place and was trying to bring her into the group. His wife was already seated in her chair and Kate wondered if she initiated the invitation so that Kate would feel welcome to join in the activities. She had always been very kind to Kate. How nice of her. She decided she would go on the hike and reciprocate their kindness in some way.

Before she reached Ken, Allen touched her arm. Ken's younger brother always surprised her because he looked so much like him.

"Kate, you absolutely must dance with me tonight," he said with a dimpled smile.

"Of course, you are such a charmer. Have you brought a date with you?"

"No, I don't have anyone to bring. Do you have a sister, perhaps?"

Laughing, she said, "No, I'm an only child. Thank you for the compliment. I will make sure to save some time on my dance card for you."

At that moment, Ken appeared at her side, putting his arm casually around her.

"It's about time for us to move to the table," he said softly to her. She moved along with him, following him to the very long oak table, at which place cards were set for each chair. She was seated next to Ken, on his right. His mother, Gwen, was already seated on her other side, which pleased her, as she got along well with her. Across from Kate sat Andrew and across from Ken, however, was Jolene. She hoped the dismay didn't show on her face. She held a firm smile on her face as she greeted her. It was going to be a long night.

The food being served was exceptional and Kate wondered who was paying for it. Did they all chip in and did Ken pay for her? Or was someone with a sizable income being very generous?

Most likely the bill was being paid by dues from the club that they all seemed to be members of.

There were numerous conversations going on but Kate couldn't engage in them since she did not know the people being discussed. Ken would talk to her now and then, although he carried on a bit with Jolene and Andrew as they talked about old times and shared experiences. Kate smiled and tried to be a gracious listener even if she could not contribute to the conversation. Gwen turned to Kate and spoke about the latest fashions.

"You must come with me to the next fashion show when we get back to London. This upcoming one will be absolutely marvelous."

"Yes, I would love to."

"Julia Aylesworth was a model. Did you know that?" she said as she looked over at the lady seated down at the other end of the table.

"Yes, I did hear. She is a beautiful woman. That doesn't surprise me in the least," Kate replied.

As Kate and Gwen continued their light social conversation, others were talking about the war clean-up efforts, while others were discussing social events and when the next party would be. No one mentioned Dexter's murder, out of politeness, Kate assumed. Thank goodness. Surely, they knew all about it by now. Did any of them suspect that she was the German National mentioned in the newspaper? They seemed to be an inquisitive crowd that thrived on gossip.

A cold cucumber soup was served, followed by a salad, asparagus, baked potatoes and roast grouse as the main course. The asparagus brought back memories of Germany. It was noticeable to everyone at the table that Kate was not engaging with the others, deep in thought, trying to focus on memories that the asparagus, the scent and the taste, brought back.

"Are you alright, dear?" Gwendolyn asked.

"Yes, fine, thank you, forgive me, what were you saying?"

"I was saying that this dinner is fabulous, don't you think?"

"Yes, it is delicious."

"The fully extravagant dinner will be tomorrow night, you are in for a treat."

"Yes, Ken told me to expect a real feast."

Kate then noticed that the conversation had turned to spy networks in England. Kate had read about them and in her position as a covert operator in Germany, must have known quite a bit about them at one time but that part of her memory had not fully come back to her. She said nothing and hoped that her face didn't reveal that her thoughts had darkened with this subject.

When dessert was served, out came the bagpipes. Five men in traditional Scottish kilts played bagpipes with a young boy banging a drum. The rendition of *Amazing Grace* brought Kate and many others almost to tears as did another song that Kate had never heard before but had a visible effect on the other guests, it was so beautifully done.

After this remarkable performance, everyone moved to the room where the dancing would be. The musicians had already been playing soft music during the meal but added a singer and a flute. They quickly switched to traditional Scottish songs with upbeat dance tempos. Men and women in traditional Scottish attire started the dancing while everyone watched.

After the traditional dance was over and the dancers bowed to applause, Ken looked at Kate questioningly and she nodded. He took her hand and the two moved out to the dance floor. Other guests joined in and dancing in earnest began. Ken kept her for the second dance as well, then Andrew tapped him on the shoulder and said it was his turn.

Whirling and smiling, Kate had a succession of dance partners, including Edward, who made her promise to agree to meet him the next morning at seven at Potter's trail, one of the many scenic hiking routes in the area. Who could resist spending time with a distinguished member of parliament and other early-rising adventurous souls? She said she would be delighted and was looking forward to seeing the beauty of Scotland and getting to know some of Ken's circle of friends. Maybe she could find something she had in common with this group of hikers.

Hopefully Ken would understand that she was being friendly, trying to fit in. Also, there was a possibility someone would reveal something that might lead to solving the two murders that she was convinced had not been resolved. After the third dance, she realized that Ken had already had too much to drink to want to rise early to go on a hike so she didn't mention it.

Allen also had his turn dancing with her, cheekily whispering in her ear several times. She giggled and whispered back. Oh, the playfulness of youth! She was happy that he had not seen the horrors of war and had a bright future ahead of him.

While Kate had been with Allen, Ken had been dancing with Jolene. They did indeed make a handsome couple and after scanning the other guests, Kate decided they were all thinking the same thing as they smiled and watched the young couple in admiration. She tried not to be caught watching them dance for fear of looking jealous. Not for the first time, she felt out of place, this time for different reasons and had just sat down for several minutes when Ken pulled her up again and the two danced a slow dance together. It was dreamy, she still felt a strong attraction to Ken. She wished she knew his feelings and if he had completely forgiven her for her mistaken accusation. How could she make it up to him?

"Ken, I can't tell you how sorry I am. I was so out of line. My imagination got the best of me. Can you forgive my unfortunate lack of judgement?"

Ken smiled. "I already have," he said quietly, whispering in her ear so that no-one could hear. "I know you were close to Dexter and to lose someone close can make you imagine things that are not true. I'm sure you relied on your imagination to survive in Germany, always anticipating the possibilities and how to talk yourself out of bad situations, if they arose."

"You are very forgiving."

"There is nothing to forgive," Ken said with his charming smile.

"How kind of you to understand," Kate spoke softly as if a heavy burden had been lifted from her shoulders. *What now?* She wondered if there was hope for them after all, at least for friendship. Could things ever be the same as they were before?

"Would you like another drink? How about a night cap in the bar area? I would love to spend some time alone with you. I want to talk to you privately."

"No, I feel one of my headaches coming on, probably too much champagne and whisky. I'm not used to all this fine food and drink. Could you just escort me back to my room?"

Ken looked disappointed.

"Okay, fine, but please make time for me tomorrow. I really want to talk to you."

"I'd like to talk to you too," Kate said, thinking that it would be best to discuss matters when they were both fully sober.

Besides her headache, Kate wanted to call it a night so that she could get plenty of sleep in preparation for the early morning hike. She wanted to keep up with everyone, who were most likely experienced hikers. Her fellow adventurers probably were all in fine shape and used to strenuous activities. Arriving at her door, Ken gave her a quick kiss on her cheek and said goodnight. Kate watched him walk down the hall to rejoin the party. She locked the door to her room as soon as she closed it, placed an angled chair beneath it, just in case. One never knew what dangerous characters could be lurking about in this far-away isolated place.

As she dressed into her night clothes and got into bed, she could hear the music again. Obviously, the party was still going full-bore and would continue into the night. Kate wondered if Ken went back to join the party. Well, why not? He had no reason not to. A single young man had every right and reason to enjoy himself at a party. She had to start thinking of and making plans for her own future.

CHAPTER 44

Kate rose early and had only a light breakfast in the dining room, picking items from the fresh buffet that was spread out along the side table. No one was there at this early hour and she thanked the kitchen staff as she turned in her plates and asked directions to the trailhead. She walked back to her room to get her backpack and bottle of water, then put on her woolen socks and hiking boots. She glanced at herself in the mirror. She certainly looked the part.

Edward was already at the trailhead and smiled when he saw her coming toward him.

"Where is everyone else?" Kate asked.

"The all bugged out. It seems they all indulged too much last night. The party lasted until the wee hours of the morning. It looks like we are the only serious true adventurers. My wife sends her regards, but she wasn't feeling well this morning. I quite honestly think she drank too much."

Kate laughed. "They certainly didn't let up on the whisky last night and I could hear the music long after I went to bed. I don't know why people would come all the way up here and not want to enjoy the great outdoors. I feel fine, although I did not over indulge. Apparently, you didn't either."

"No, I knew I needed to stay focused."

"Stay focused on what?"

"On the beauty and magic of Scotland. I've got some fantastic views picked out for this morning. You're in for a treat."

"It's a lovely morning, Mr. Aylesworth," she said, anxious for a brisk walk. "Thanks for inviting me. We'll let the others know what they missed when we come back tired but exhilarated."

"Please call me Edward."

He took off on the trail heading north and Kate followed. The path went through a little birch grove toward a river. His pace was quite fast. They were steadily climbing a steep path and she was soon out of breath.

"Edward, could you slow down a bit?" She had been hoping for an enjoyable, brisk but casual walk, but it wasn't turning out to be much fun, it seemed more like a march.

"Of course, Kate, but there's something I want you to see and it's best to see it early in the morning."

She continued following as quickly as she could, trying to remember which turns he was taking in case they got lost or she lost him, which seemed likely considering how fast he was moving.

After what seemed like several miles on this remote stretch of path, all of a sudden he stopped, and she came up behind him. They were at a clearing on the top of a mountainside, looking down a steep valley, composed entirely of brownish rocks striated with shades of gray and blue. At the bottom was a rushing river, sparkling as droplets bounced off boulders, clear cobalt blue, flowing rapidly along.

"It's beautiful!" Kate exclaimed. Noticing there was a bench to the left, which must have been placed there for hikers to enjoy the view, she sat down, hoping to catch her breath.

Edward sat next to her.

"How much of your memory has come back?" he said in German, looking out in the distance.

This startled Kate. What he said and that he said it in German raised a multitude of questions in her mind. His words created an atmosphere of darkness and treachery that hung in this beautiful setting.

"Excuse me?" she said in English.

"Kate, I know all about you, your amnesia, that you are German, and what you have done."

"I'm sorry, I really don't know what nonsense you're talking about."

Kate's guard was up and she debated how quickly she could jump up from the bench and run away from him. How could this man know anything about her?

"Dexter told me everything, foolish man. He never could hold his drink and he talked when he had too much." Edward said thoughtfully, "Good thing he was never a spy."

Silence. They could hear the rushing water of the river below them.

"Oh God, it's you," Kate said.

Edward looked tired, as if he were tired of the lying and the constant effort it took to try to escape his past. Kate closed her eyes and took a slow long breath.

"If you didn't recognize me now, I knew you would eventually," he said in an ice cold voice. "I could see recognition in your eyes last night during dinner and when spy networks were mentioned. I watched your face closely. You probably did fool most of our group by your story of being an innocent English country girl but I had suspicions about you from the start. Dexter confirmed that you were an Allied agent stationed in Germany, after more than a few drinks,"

Kate didn't answer, her mind was moving through a million hurdles at this point as she struggled to gain some ground with him and her precarious situation. A chill went through her as she recognized the danger she was in. She realized that on this remote stretch of path there was no one near enough to hear her call and that he had planned this carefully, meticulously, and she again had walked into one of his traps. There had never been anyone else invited on this country walk.

"Yes, you're right. I do remember seeing a photograph of you when I worked undercover at Intelligence in Germany. You were involved in the spy ring in Worcestershire. One of our Allied operatives was assigned undercover to learn about your group and never returned."

She realized she was sitting on a bench, all alone, with the man who killed Natalie and Dexter. Now, Kate guessed, she was the only loose end. She tried not to look down from the cliff. After all she had been through and survived against all odds, she was not about to let this be the end for her. She had been taught self-defense before she left on her covert mission in Germany. And yet, this man, high up on a mountain, had been calculating his course of action. It seemed important not to show fear, to stall him in conversation while she thought up a plan of action.

"Ken will never believe that I fell off a cliff, if that's your plan. He will be suspicious and he will be very thorough in researching your past, and will uncover your dark secrets."

"You overestimate Ken's concern for you. Don't you know that most of my group, including Ken, believe you killed Dexter and think that hussy, Jolene, killed Natalie. Everyone assumes you were sleeping with Dexter. They will accept your unfortunate accident. And you clearly overestimate Ken's ability to find out anything about me."

"He knows I was an allied spy. He'll put the pieces together."

"We'll see. You are not the only one who can act. You lost your footing, there was nothing I could do. My reputation is beyond reproach. The authorities will never doubt my word."

Stall, just stall, Kate thought. She noticed the slightest tremor shook her hand and her pulse was racing. "So that's how you got away with it, your reputation. How could you turn your back on England, your country?"

"What about you? Didn't you turn your back on your country?"

"I worked against the Third Reich, but I was loyal to Germany, the Germany I knew and loved, my home."

"England should have negotiated with Hitler and not gone to war. My economic interests in Germany had to be protected. The war has wiped me out. I am nearly broke."

"There is no negotiating with pure evil. So, it was all about money with you."

"Everything is all about money! You are so naïve. It's about time you learned the truth – about life and about people. When it comes down to it, my dear, that's what matters to everyone.

People only care about being on the winning side and how it will benefit them."

"You are wrong." She felt her words had affected him since he had to justify himself and his actions. To keep him talking was her only chance. "Tell that to the families of the men and women who lost their lives on the battlefields. There is such a thing as honor and loyalty."

This hit home with Edward and seemed to strike a nerve. He reached for her arm and held it in a vice-like grip. Kate realized she could not overpower him as he started to lift her off the bench.

"How could you kill Natalie, you had known her since the day she was born."

"Don't waste sympathy for Natalie. She broke into my study and rifled through my desk to find my personal papers. I don't know what tipped her off. She had no right to do that. She took my book of contacts and I had to get that back. Then Dexter told me he had found a key to a safe deposit box that Natalie had given him and was going to check it out. Thank God I gave him the ride home that night. I knew it might contain information about me. I had to silence him."

Just at that moment, a large bird swooped down and landed next to them on a branch. The noise startled Edward and he quickly turned to see if someone was there, afraid there might be a witness to what was being said. As he did, he loosened his grip. This was her one opportunity to escape. She broke free from his grasp with strength she didn't know she possessed and jumped away from him, running into the trees, away from the cliff, zigzagging her course. Later, she would think that the bird was her guardian angel.

She heard a shot whiz by, but it missed her because she had just tripped on a tree branch and had fallen to the ground. She fell on her wrist and realized it was hurt, sprained or broken. The pain was debilitating but masked by the adrenalin running through her as she knew she had little time to get away. Of course he would have a gun, thought Kate, in case he had failed to push me off the cliff. Not as convenient as a fall down a cliff, but he could come up with a story that the gun went off accidently. It would only make sense to carry a gun with him in the wilderness, no one would question that. She heard his footsteps behind her coming closer.

With newfound strength and determination, she jumped up and continued running an almost-crash course, jumping this way and that way, hoping she wouldn't be in his sights long enough for him to aim and shoot again.

Always a nimble sprinter, she was able to gain some ground, put some distance between them. She heard him curse as he stumbled on the same tree branch that she had tripped over. Hopefully he was hurt, maybe he broke his leg so that he would be unable to continue the chase. Either way, hurt or not, with the few moments of delay, she could increase the space between them. She continued running as fast as she could, turning back occasionally and eventually not seeing or hearing him.

After what seemed like hours, she stopped behind a tree and listened. Not a sound. She was quite out of breath but kept as quiet as she could. Unfortunately, she was lost. It was a lovely place to be lost in, but not when she was fearing for her life.

CHAPTER 45

Breakfast at the Inn was a group affair, with a delicious buffet offering everything a person could possibly want to eat or drink. Most of the group had overindulged the night before and slept late. Now they were able to enjoy the food and strong cups of coffee.

Ken wondered where Kate was. He had knocked on her door this morning and she didn't answer. He noticed Julia sitting by herself at a table.

"Mind if I join you?"

"That would be delightful."

"Where is Edward this morning?"

"He said he was going for a hike. I offered to join him but he said he wanted some time alone. That's fine with me, I enjoyed sleeping late and I am thoroughly enjoying this scrumptious breakfast and sorely-needed coffee."

Ken finished his food after light conversation and said goodbye to Julia. He still could not imagine where Kate could be and was starting to get worried. He went up to her room and knocked on the door again. No answer. Seeing a maid walking down the hall, he caught her and asked if she would open the room for him, as he'd forgotten his key. She complied and left to continue her work. Looking inside her room, he noticed the bed was made. He opened the closet door and saw that her outdoor clothing was gone. Also gone was her backpack. His concern turned to alarm.

CHAPTER 46

Sitting down for a minute to catch her breath, Kate pulled out the bottle of water from her backpack and took a drink. She considered her surroundings. Thank goodness it wasn't raining. It was before noon, so the sun would be in the east, which was behind her right now. That meant she had likely run several miles to the west. Turning to her left, she also figured that heading down the hill would eventually lead to a road or maybe somewhere close to the Inn.

Slowly moving in a southern direction, she marched along, her wrist aching, stopping behind trees as often as possible, just as a precaution. Her pace was slow but steady. She could hear no sounds behind her but that didn't remove the strong sense of fear. She couldn't completely let down her guard even though it looked like she may have outmaneuvered her pursuer.

After what seemed like ages she saw an answer to her prayers - the trees thinning and green fields ahead. She had to run across an open field with no cover or protection to reach what looked like a road ahead.

Please God, don't let him see me, don't let him shoot me.

She used every ounce of strength she had to quickly clear the field. Nearing the dirt road, she positioned herself behind a large bush, and listening carefully, waited for a car to drive by so that she could wave the driver down.

It wasn't long before she heard a vehicle approach and ran out to the middle of the road, waving the arm that was not injured and yelling for help. She recognized the car as belonging to the lodge. The driver was Ken. He slowed down and opened the door, quickly getting out and walking toward her.

"Kate, we've been searching for you. Where have you been?"

Still out of breath, she ran into his arms. Above the hillside, they both heard the faint sound of a gun going off. They looked toward the sound and then at each other. The look in his eyes was evident to Kate that Ken had an idea of what had transpired. She nodded, "Yes, it's what you think."

"Edward?"

"Yes."

Then he noticed that she was holding her wrist. "Are you hurt?"

"Yes, I fell. I tripped over a log. I think it's either sprained or broken."

He put his arm around her. "We need to take care of that immediately.' He gently helped her into the passenger side and drove to the lodge at breakneck speed. She didn't say a word, just leaned her head against the back of the seat with her eyes closed. *Thank God it's over.*

CHAPTER 47

When Julia found out what had happened on the mountain, she was sad, but relieved. She now realized her suspicions were true. She had falsely given Edward an alibi to the authorities the night that Natalie was murdered. He was not home with her but asked her to lie for him. He said he had fallen asleep at his office but there was no one there to see him so he didn't have an alibi and didn't want the police to suspect him. He was so charming that she thought nothing of it. She had no reason to suspect him of the terrible crime.

Through the war years, things started to add up and her suspicions grew. By the time of the Allied victory, she had become convinced that he was involved in something treasonous. Not wanting to believe it, but concerned about what might happen, she called Scotland Yard anonymously to say she knew who killed Natalie and that the person would strike again. She was hoping The Yard would be more aggressive in their investigations after her call. She was prepared to tell the truth - if they had asked her – that Edward was not home on the night of Natalie's murder.

In the last few weeks, Edward had spent a lot of time with Dexter. There had to be a reason why and she knew that Dexter was close to Natalie and that he was working on a story of espionage. When Dexter was murdered, she was pretty certain he had been involved. It had been hard to act happy and carefree around her husband, and she was afraid that he would snap at any time and possibly harm her as well. She was afraid to go the authorities, as he was very controlling and seemed to watch her every move.

Overall, she felt a sense of relief, now that he was gone. He had taken the only way out he could, an ending she feared would eventually happen. He would never have allowed himself to be arrested and tried.

She said a prayer of thanks that Kate had survived the final treacherous plans of her late husband.

CHAPTER 48

Back at the lodge, Ken helped Kate up to her room, settling her down on the bed. Kate gave him a weak smile and was finally able to take a deep breath. Her wrist was throbbing.

"I'm calling the police and for medical help right now," he said as he opened the door to his adjoining room. He made several phone calls.

It wasn't long before a kind-looking man arrived with a medical bag.

"Let's see what we have here," he said as he took her arm and started to exam her wrist. He determined it was a sprain.

"Thank God it's not broken," Ken said.

The doctor asked for ice to be brought up and made a sling for her, putting it on gently. He gave her some pain pills which she decided not to take. He said they would make her drowsy and she knew she still had to give her statement to the police and wanted to be completely alert.

Ken went down to the kitchen and came back with an ice pack and something to eat. A maid followed him in the room with tea.

"Here, put this ice on your wrist," Ken said as he handed her the ice pack.

"Thank you, I'm not very hungry, but that tea is a welcome sight."

The maid poured her a cup and then left the room. As Kate sipped tea, somewhat awkwardly as she had to use her left hand instead of her right, she explained to Ken about Edward's invitation and the morning's events. She told him all that Edward had confessed to her.

"My God, I would never have suspected him, of all people."

Then Ken was summoned downstairs. Within ten minutes, he came back up to Kate and told her what they had already surmised, that Edward had shot himself. They'd found his body. He had hurt his leg on the branch which explained why Kate was able to out-run him. The policeman then came in her room to take her statement.

Ken stayed in the room and listened to the interrogation. Kate gave a concise account of the events of the morning. The policeman took notes and listened intently. After he was satisfied that all his questions were answered, and he had a complete statement, he asked her to sign it, which she did. He thanked her and took his leave.

"How do you feel?" Ken asked.

"Much better. The ice has brought down the swelling a little and it's helped with the pain. I guess it's time to go downstairs and join the crowd. What do you think?"

"I think that's a good idea."

The guests had been informed of what had happened. In the main meeting room, much of their party were gathered. Several of them were comforting Julia and others ran to Kate's side to inquire about how she was holding up. Kate reassured them that she was fine. They all seemed to be in shock at Edward's suicide and the other, more horrifying implications of what the man had been involved in. They spoke amongst themselves in muted tones.

CHAPTER 49

Ken suggested to Kate that the two of them might want to take a walk down a path he knew of that led through some trees. Kate put her jacket over her shoulders and agreed that might be a good idea. Some fresh air would do her well.

"What a nasty business," Ken said once the two were outside and alone.

"Yes, it's horrible that he had to murder to cover up his dark secrets. Well, at least now we know that he killed Natalie and her murder is solved, I am so sorry it turned out to be a trusted friend."

"He killed Dexter as well. I know you were fond of him. I'm sorry I got you involved in all of this."

Kate chose not to respond to his comment about Dexter. "I volunteered to help, and now I am happy that you and your family can have some closure, maybe some peace, although I know it won't bring Natalie back. I've spent so much time learning about her and reading her newspaper submissions, I feel as though I knew her. She was a brave woman, not unlike you, who risked her life for her country."

"I wonder how Natalie started to suspect Edward."

"I don't know. Something must have alerted her, or she overheard something. Perhaps she walked in on him at his house when he was on the phone in a secluded room."

"What was that letter about, then? The one that Dexter wrote to Natalie?"

Kate explained to him what her theory was regarding the letter and the meaning of it. Then she added more of her ideas. "I've been trying to reconstruct what happened that night in my mind. I suppose Dexter went to see her and she did not answer the door because she had already been killed. Perhaps Edward was still in the house when Dexter came calling. The murder must have piqued Dexter's interest, but Edward had taken all of Natalie's papers and retrieved his book of contacts."

"What a false friend we've spent time with all these years."

"I guess he was the lost dark spy, the one that slipped through the cracks. I recall reading that all the other Worcestershire spy ring participants have been found and tried. He was very cunning and ruthlessly killed anyone that ever suspected him. Always one step ahead of the game."

"Did you ever suspect him?"

"No, there is a slight chance I would have recognized him when my memory came back entirely. Hearing his voice on the mountain and with what he was saying, I vaguely remembered seeing a photo of him one time in Germany and I'm sure I heard his name when I was there. Since Dexter told him all about me, Edward must have known I would identify him eventually"

"Thank God I came when I did."

"Yes, that's twice that you have saved me. Thank you."

"The least I could do for the risk you took to save me and my men back in Germany. You put your life on the line for us. I have only done what anyone would do when I rescued you."

Kate smiled at the thought that these men were back safe in England.

"I brought you here to enjoy yourself and forget about your problems. They have seemed to follow you here."

The last comment reminded her of the conversation she had witnessed the night before and she said, "Ken, now that you've mentioned problems, there's something I overheard last night that I need to tell you about."

"What is it?"

"You better take a deep breath."

"Okay, fine, now tell me."

"Tell your cousin Amanda that her son is alive and well and in a boarding school in Switzerland. I was going to tell her first thing on my return back to London."

Ken stopped in his tracks, gasped and stared at Kate.

"You can't be serious."

"Yes, I'm sure of it."

"How on earth did you....?"

"I overheard Mr. Patel talking to a man in the cigar bar. They were speaking in French and never guessed that I was fluent in the language. Why would they?"

"My God. I didn't know that she confided in you that she had once had a baby."

"She told me all about it. Thank God she did, or I wouldn't have known what the two gentlemen were referring to. Amanda and I have confided a lot in each other. She felt comfortable enough to share her past with me and I'm so glad I've found out the truth. And Amanda now has leverage over the Patels for what they have done...and since Raj is not married yet...maybe she and Raj and Daniel could be a family."

Ken was speechless. Then he said, "If I don't kill Raj and his parents first. Wait till I get my hands on them. I'll wring their bloody necks."

"You won't do anything of the sort. Hear me out. I thought about this all night. Amanda and Raj still care for each other. And apparently Daniel is a happy, intelligent and engaging child. I'm sure he will be thrilled to be reunited with his 'sister' and be part of a family with her and Raj. Think about Daniel before you take any actions, he has to be the main focus now, his happiness has to trump everything else."

"Surely this would have come out at some time."

"Yes, it surely would. They will claim they only did it to save Daniel during the blitz and not knowing what the outcome of the war was going to be. Who knows? Maybe they did save his life by getting him out of London during the German airstrikes. They managed to get him into a boarding school in the neutral country of Switzerland where he would be safe. They did not have malicious intent, they just wanted to protect him, I'm sure. You have to admit that things looked bleak at one time for England. It would have been reasonable to assume that there was a strong possibility England could have been lost to Nazi Germany." Kate was so relieved that Amanda's son was alive and well that she couldn't think too badly of the Patels. She thought Amanda would react the same way.

"Yes, that is true."

"The Patels and others underestimated Churchill."

"And they underestimated people like us."

"Yes, they certainly did."

"So, what then would have been their plan, I wonder."

"If England had fallen, I'm guessing they could have raised Daniel in India," Kate surmised.

"If you must defend them, I guess you do have a point."

"I think Raj meant to tell Amanda everything. He ran into her at the market, probably followed her there. She said he was trying desperately to tell her something, but she ran out of the store, not wanting to hear anything he had to say."

"Amanda will be overwhelmed with joy. We all will. I would like you to give her this life-altering news yourself. Let's leave for London tonight, or tomorrow morning at the latest."

"No, Ken, I think I should get out of your life, the sooner the better, and make a life for myself. I've overstayed my welcome with you and Fred. The mysteries are solved."

Her statement brought on a few moments of silence. They could hear the branches break under their feet as they walked along.

Kate finally spoke what was on her mind, "Isn't that why you brought me here, Ken? Isn't that why you brought me to London in the first place, thinking my memory would come back and I would recognize someone that would help you find the killer?"

"No, that is not why I invited you to London. And that is not why I invited you here, not at all. You are entirely on the wrong track."

"Why did you invite me here?"

Without answering, Ken asked, "What are your plans now?"

"I think I would like to teach at the university. Mr. Robertson said I could now become a British citizen and he would help me work on getting my teaching certification and assist me in obtaining a position. Classes will start soon so I can't delay. I want to devote my life to educating people so there is never another war like the one we just witnessed."

"That is a noble cause indeed."

Kate looked at Ken and smiled.

He looked down for a moment. Then he looked her in the eyes and slowly said, as if he were trying to find the right words. "I have meant to ask you for a long time – were you in love with Dexter?"

"I don't know. I certainly admired him and I guess I was flattered by his attention. Why do you ask? What does it matter to you?"

Ken continued, "It matters to me because, although your plans are admirable and I support them fully, there is something else I wish you would consider in your future plans."

"What's that?"

"Becoming my wife."

"What?" Kate immediately said and looked at him with widened eyes. Certainly, she could not have heard him correctly

"I'm serious, Kate"

Looking at him, wondering where this proposal was coming from, she managed to stumble out some words.

"I thought you only regarded me as a friend."

"Well I tried to show you my affection, but I was rebuffed. You thought I was a murderer at the time."

Kate could not help but laugh. "Please do not remind me. I don't know how I could have been so misguided."

"What do you say about my proposal? That is why I invited you here, Kate, to propose for real. That's why I wanted to talk to you privately. Then I was hoping, if you consented, to announce our wedding date at tonight's dinner. And you already have the ring," Ken said with a Cheshire cat smile.

"That's why you invited me here? Is this true?"

"Yes."

"Ken, you don't have to marry me under any obligation. I saved your life, you saved mine, twice. We are even. You owe me nothing."

"This has nothing to do with anyone owing anything. I love you, you know," he said simply and continued. "I believe that you saved my life twice. In Germany and then back home when I finally realized what love is. And you?"

"I love you," she said, without hesitancy. "But….."

"What now?"

"Ken, I saw you with Jolene. The night after the Ness Hotel party, at your uncle's home, after everyone had gone to bed."

"Oh that. She cornered me and she kissed me. I was more kissed than kissing. Believe me, I broke away from her as soon as I could and sent her home. Did you really think I was involved with her?"

"Yes, I did. She is a beautiful woman."

"I have never been in love with her. I consider her a friend. I made that clear to her after that night. Besides, she and Andrew are an item once again. I expect him to propose to her at any time now."

"That's what Amanda said. Why did everyone know that but me?"

"You didn't know? What kind of spy are you?'

Kate smiled, "Very funny, I just assumed…"

"Well, what do you say? Marry me." He stopped, faced her, put her hand in his and held it.

"But what will your family say? We are from vastly different classes."

"They will be greatly disappointed in me…"

Kate looked down at the ground understanding what she thought he was saying, but Ken continued, "If I don't bring you back to the party and announce a date."

She looked at him with an expression in her eyes of elation and growing excitement at his sincerity and the thought that her love for him was actually being returned.

"They all adore you, surely you know that. Anna would never speak to me again if I didn't marry you. So, what do you say?"

"Yes, Ken, I would be happy and honored to marry you."

"Absolutely grand," he said as he put his arm around her and they continued their walk further down the path.

After a moment, Ken stopped and looked at her. "Of course, I may not kiss as well as Dexter."

Kate blushed, "Oh, you heard about that."

"My Aunt Margaret saw you at the Ness Hotel. You can be sure all of London heard about it. Maybe all of Britain."

"No wonder it got back to Fred and Robertson," Kate said with a knowing smile. "You can trust me that it was the same situation as you and Jolene. I guess we are both irresistible."

"Water under the bridge."

"Perhaps we could have a double wedding with Amanda and Raj."

"What makes you think Amanda would take Raj back? Do you think she could forgive him for the deception he and his family have been a part of?"

"I do. She is a kind and forgiving spirit. And she loves Raj, otherwise she would be engaged by now. She has had no scarcity of suitors. Raj could convince her that he thought Daniel was in imminent danger. Amanda loves him, and you know what they say – love conquers all."

"There is too much scandal with those two, if they marry, it will be a quiet, private service. If, and only if, Amanda would consider it." Ken looked at her, trying to read her thoughts. "We can have an elaborate affair, no expenses spared. Isn't that what you would want?"

"Do you think there is no scandal with the both of us? We've both been seen romantically involved with other people. Your Aunt Margaret and others would only come to our wedding out of curiosity and to enjoy the salacious gossip for years to come. I could not bear the awkward silence when the minister will say 'If anyone objects'."

Ken didn't know what to say. He knew there were some relatives who wouldn't be pleased with their marriage, but the close circle of friends and family were supportive. Especially after Kate had put her life on the line in her pursuit of helping to solve Natalie's murder. Not to mention saving his men in Germany. The war again, the bloody war. It affected everything. The world would not be exactly the same as it was before, but love, courage and dedication remained and always would. The human spirit, defiant of evil, would always prevail. Of that he was certain and that was what mattered most.

"Whatever you want will be fine with me and my family."

"You know, I would prefer a quiet, private service in a small church with immediate family."

"This is one of the many things I love about you, Kate. Most women would want an elaborate wedding, the most formal and expensive affair. Nothing but the best and you know my family could afford it. But you look to the heart of the matter."

"There is much I love about you as well. Not just the big things, but the little things that you do."

"It's settled then, let's set a date."

"Are you completely sure you have thought this through and this is truly what you want, Ken? I don't come from the social class that a man in your position would want and need a wife to have."

Ken rolled his eyes, this was getting tedious, "Please stop arguing with me, Kate."

He turned to face her again and pulled her close to him. "Kiss me instead." And she did, and it was so right.

THE AUTHORS

Joan Carson

Born and raised in Denver, Colorado, Joan Carson-Schoepflin is an alumna of Colorado University at Denver with two career passions, writing mysteries and accounting. The author of *Lost Contact*, she is blessed to have the talented Pamela Curtiss as a co-writer on this novel. She lives in Denver, Colorado with her husband, Stephen Schoepflin.

Pamela Curtiss

A writer and song-composer since age 13, Pamela Curtiss has a varied background which includes technical writing, owning and operating a sign shop and newspaper reporting. She lives in a small town on Colorado's Western Slope. This is her first foray into writing mysteries, and she is honored to work with long-time friend Joan Carson.

www.ingramcontent.com/pod-product-compliance
Lightning Source LLC
Chambersburg PA
CBHW060916250626
47159CB00008B/3032